SCHO

GHO
STORIES

SCHOLASTIC
New York Toronto London Auckland
Sydney New Delhi Hong Kong

Published by Scholastic India Pvt. Ltd.
A subsidiary of Scholastic Inc., New York, 10012 (USA).
Publishers since 1920, with international operations in Canada,
Australia, New Zealand, the United Kingdom, India, and Hong Kong.

For information regarding permission, write to:
Scholastic India Pvt. Ltd.
A-27, Ground Floor, Bharti Sigma Centre
Infocity-1, Sector 34, Gurgaon-122001 (India)

First edition: April 2018, Oct. 2018

ISBN-13: 978-93-5275-404-5

Printed at MicroPrints (India), New Delhi

CONTENTS

HIS DEAD WIFE'S PHOTOGRAPH

S Mukherji

This story created a sensation when it was first told. It appeared in the papers and many big physicists and natural philosophers were, at least so they thought, able to explain the phenomenon. I shall narrate the event and also tell the reader what explanation was given, and let him draw his own conclusions.

This was what happened.

***

A friend of mine, a clerk in the same office as myself, was an amateur photographer; let us call him Jones.

Jones had a half plate Sanderson camera with a Ross lens and a Thornton Picard behind lens shutter, with pneumatic release. The plate in question was a Wrattens ordinary, developed with Ilford Pyro Soda developer prepared at home. All these particulars I give for the benefit of the more technical reader.

Mr Smith, another clerk in our office, invited Mr Jones to take a likeness of his wife and sister-in-law.

This sister-in-law was the wife of Mr Smith's elder brother, who was also a Government servant, then on leave. The idea of the photograph was of the sister-in-law.

Jones was a keen photographer himself. He had photographed everybody in the office including the peons and sweepers, and had even supplied every sitter of his with copies of his handiwork. So he most willingly consented, and anxiously waited for the Sunday on which the photograph was to be taken.

Early on Sunday morning, Jones went to the Smiths'. The arrangement of light in the verandah was such that a photograph could only be taken after midday; and so he stayed there to breakfast.

At about one in the afternoon, all arrangements were complete and the two ladies, Mrs Smiths, were made to sit in two cane chairs and after long and careful focussing, and moving the camera about for an hour, Jones was satisfied at last and an exposure was made. Mr Jones was sure that the plate was all right; and so, a second plate was not exposed although in the usual course of things this should have been done.

He wrapped up his things and went home promising to develop the plate the same night and bring a copy of the photograph the next day to the office.

The next day, which was a Monday, Jones came to the office very early, and I was the first person to meet him.

'Well, Mr Photographer,' I asked, 'what success?'

'I got the picture all right,' said Jones, unwrapping an

unmounted picture and handing it over to me 'most funny,
don't you think so?'

'No, I don't ... I think it is all right, at any rate I did not
expect anything better from you ...' I said.

'No,' said Jones 'the funny thing is that only two ladies
sat ...'

'Quite right,' I said 'the third stood in the middle.'

'There was no third lady at all there ...' said Jones.

'Then you imagined she was there, and there we find her ...'

'I tell you, there were only two ladies there when I exposed,'
insisted Jones. He was looking awfully worried.

'Do you want me to believe that there were only two
persons when the plate was exposed and three when it was
developed?' I asked.

'That is exactly what has happened,' said Jones.

'Then it must be the most wonderful developer you used,
or was it that this was the second exposure given to the same
plate?'

'The developer is the one which I have been using for the
last three years, and the plate, the one I charged on Saturday
night out of a new box that I had purchased only on Saturday
afternoon.'

A number of other clerks had come up in the meantime,
and were taking great interest in the picture and in Jones'
statement.

It is only right that a description of the picture be given
here for the benefit of the reader. I wish I could reproduce the
original picture too, but that for certain reasons is impossible.

When the plate was actually exposed there were only two
ladies, both of whom were sitting in cane chairs. When the

...te was developed it was found that there was in the picture a figure, that of a lady, standing in the middle.

She wore a broad-edged *dhoti* (the reader should not forget that all the characters are Indians), only the upper half of her body being visible, the lower being covered up by the low backs of the cane chairs. She was distinctly behind the chairs, and consequently slightly out of focus. Still everything was quite clear. Even her long necklace was visible through the little opening in the *dhoti* near the right shoulder. She was resting her hands on the backs of the chairs and the fingers were nearly totally out of focus, but a ring on the right ring-finger was clearly visible.

She looked like a handsome young woman of twenty-two, short and thin. One of the earrings was also clearly visible, although the face itself was slightly out of focus. One thing, and probably the funniest thing, that we overlooked then but observed afterwards, was that immediately behind the three ladies was a barred window. The two ladies, who were one on each side, covered up the bars to a certain height from the bottom with their bodies, but the lady in the middle was partly transparent because the bars of the window were very faintly visible through her. This fact, however, as I have said already, we did not observe then. We only laughed at Jones and tried to assure him that he was either drunk or asleep. At this moment Smith of our office walked in, removing the trouser clips from his legs.

Smith took the unmounted photograph, looked at it for a minute, turned red and blue and green and finally very pale. Of course, we asked him what the matter was and this was what he said:

'The third lady in the middle was my first wife, who has been dead these eight years. Before her death she asked me a number of times to have her photograph taken. She used to say that she had a presentiment that she might die early. I did not believe in her presentiment myself, but I did not object to the photograph. So one day I ordered the carriage and asked her to dress up. We intended to go to a good professional. She dressed up and the carriage was ready, but as we were going to start news reached us that her mother was dangerously ill. So we went to see her mother instead. The mother was very ill, and I had to leave her there.

Immediately afterwards I was sent away on duty to another station and so could not bring her back. It was in fact after full three months and a half that I returned and then though her mother was all right, my wife was not. Within fifteen days of my return she died of puerperal fever after child-birth and the child died too. A photograph of her was never taken. When she dressed up for the last time on the day that she left my home she had the necklace and the earrings on, as you see her wearin꜀ in the photograph. My present wife has them now but she does not generally put them on.'

This was too big a pill for me to swallow. So I at once took French leave from my office, bagged the photograph and rushed out on my bicycle. I went to Mr Smith's house and looked Mrs Smith up. Of course, si.꜀ was much astonished to see a third lady in the picture but could not guess who she was. This I had expected, as supposing Smith's story to be true, this lady had never seen her husband's first wife.

The elder brother's wife, however, recognised the likeness at once and she virtually repeated the story which Smith had told me earlier that day. She even brought out the necklace and the earrings for my inspection and conviction. They were the same as those in the photograph.

All the principal newspapers of that time got hold of the fact and within a week there was any number of applications for the ghostly photograph. But Mr Jones refused to supply copies of it to anybody for various reasons, the principal being that Smith would not allow it. I am, however, the fortunate possessor of a copy which, for obvious reasons, I am not allowed to show to anybody. One copy of the picture was sent to America and another to England. I do not now remember exactly to whom. My own copy I showed to the Rev Father— MA, DSC, BD, etc., and asked him to find out a scientific explanation of the phenomenon. The following explanation was given by the gentleman. (I am afraid I shall not be able to reproduce the learned Father's exact words, but this is what he meant or at least what I understood him to mean.)

'The girl in question was dressed in this particular way on an occasion, say ten years ago. Her image was cast *on space* and the reflection was projected from one luminous body (one planet) on another till it made a circuit of millions and millions of miles in space and then came back to earth at the exact moment when our friend, Mr Jones, was going to make the exposure.'

'Take for instance the case of a man who is taking the photograph of a mirage. He is photographing place X from place Y, when X and Y are, say, 200 miles apart, and it may be that his camera is facing east while place X is actually towards the west of place Y.'

In school I had read a little of Science and Chemistry and

could make a dry analysis of a salt; but this was an item too big for my limited comprehension.

The fact, however, remains and I believe it, that Smith's first wife did come back to this terrestrial globe of ours over eight years after her death to give a sitting for a photograph in a form which, though it did not affect the retina of our eye, did impress a sensitised plate; in a form that did not affect the retina of the eye, I say, because Jones must have been looking at his sitters at the time when he was pressing the bulb of the pneumatic release of his time and instantaneous shutter.

The story is most wonderful but this is exactly what happened. Smith says this is the first time he has ever seen, or heard from, his dead wife.

It is popularly believed in India that a dead wife gives a lot of trouble, if she ever revisits this earth, but this is, thank god, not the experience of my friend, Mr Smith.

It is now over seven years since the event mentioned above happened; and the dead girl has never appeared again. I would very much like to have a photograph of the two ladies taken once more; but I have never ventured to approach Smith with the proposal.

In fact, I learnt photography myself with a view to take the photograph of the two ladies, but as I have said, I have never been able to speak to Smith about my intention, and probably never shall. The £10 that I spent on my cheap photographic outfit may be a waste. But I have learnt an art which though rather costly for my limited means is nevertheless an art worth learning.

A SCHOOL STORY

M R James

Two men in a smoking-room were talking of their private-school days. 'At our school,' said A, 'we had a ghost's footmark on the staircase. What was it like? Oh, very unconvincing. Just the shape of a shoe, with a square toe, if I remember right. The staircase was a stone one. I never heard any story about the thing. That seems odd, when you come to think of it. Why didn't somebody invent one, I wonder?'

'You never can tell with little boys. They have a mythology of their own. There's a subject for you, by the way "The Folklore of Private Schools".'

'Yes; the crop is rather scanty, though. I imagine, if you were to investigate the cycle of ghost stories, for instance, which the boys at private schools tell each other, they would all turn out to be highly-compressed versions of stories out of books.'

'Nowadays the Strand and Pearson's, and so on, would be extensively drawn upon.'

'No doubt: they weren't born or thought of in my time. Let's see. I wonder if I can remember the staple ones that I was told. First, there was the house with a room in which a series of people insisted on passing a night; and each of them in the morning was found kneeling in a corner, and had just time to say, "I've seen it," and died.'

'Wasn't that the house in Berkeley Square?'

'I dare say it was. Then there was the man who heard a noise in the passage at night, opened his door, and saw someone crawling towards him on all fours with his eye hanging out on his cheek. There was besides, let me think, yes! The room where a man was found dead in bed with a horseshoe mark on his forehead, and the floor under the bed was covered with marks of horseshoes also; I don't know why. Also there was the lady who, on locking her bedroom door in a strange house, heard a thin voice among the bed-curtains say, "Now we're shut in for the night." None of those had any explanation or sequel. I wonder if they go on still, those stories.'

'Oh, likely enough—with additions from the magazines, as I said. You never heard, did you, of a real ghost at a private school? I thought not; nobody has that ever I came across.'

'From the way in which you said that, I gather that you have.'

'I really don't know; but this is what was in my mind. It happened at my private school thirty odd years ago, and I haven't any explanation of it.'

'The school I mean was near London. It was established in a large and fairly old house a great white building with very fine grounds about it; there were large cedars in the garden, as there are in so many of the older gardens in the Thames valley, and ancient elms in the three or four fields which we used for our games. I think probably it was quite an attractive place, but boys seldom allow that their schools possess any tolerable features.'

'I came to the school in a September, soon after the year 1870; and among the boys who arrived on the same day was one whom I took to: a Highland boy, whom I will call McLeod. I needn't spend time in describing him: the main thing is that I got to know him very well. He was not an exceptional boy in any way not particularly good at books or games but he suited me.'

'The school was a large one: there must have been from 120 to 130 boys there as a rule, and so a considerable staff of masters was required, and there were rather frequent changes among them.'

'One term, perhaps it was my third or fourth, a new master made his appearance. His name was Sampson. He was a tallish, stoutish, pale, black-bearded man. I think we liked him: he had travelled a good deal, and had stories which amused us on our school walks, so that there was some competition among us to get within earshot of him. I remember, too, dear me, I have hardly thought of it since then that he had a charm on his watch-chain that attracted my attention one day, and he let me examine it. It was, I now suppose, a gold Byzantine coin; there was an effigy of some absurd emperor on one side; the other side had been worn practically smooth, and he had had cut on it rather barbarously his own initials, GWS, and a date, July 24, 1865. Yes, I can see it now: he told me he had picked it up in Constantinople: it was about the size of a florin, perhaps rather smaller.'

'Well, the first odd thing that happened was this. Sampson was doing Latin grammar with us. One of his favourite methods, perhaps it is rather a good one, was to make us construct sentences out of our own heads to illustrate the rules he was trying to make us learn. Of course, that is a thing which gives a silly boy a chance of being impertinent: there are lots of school stories in which that happens or anyhow there might be. But Sampson was too good a disciplinarian for us to think of trying that on with him.'

'Now, on this occasion he was telling us how to express remembering in Latin: and he ordered us each to make a sentence bringing in the verb memini, "I remember". Well, most of us made up some ordinary sentence such as "I remember my father", or "He remembers his book", or something equally uninteresting: and I dare say a good many put down *memino librum meum*, and so forth: but the boy I mentioned—McLeod, was evidently thinking of something more elaborate than that. The rest of us wanted to have our sentences passed, and get on to something else, so some kicked him under the desk, and I, who was next to him, poked him and whispered to him to look sharp. But he didn't seem to attend. I looked at his paper and saw he had put down nothing at all.'

'So I jogged him again harder than before and upbraided him sharply for keeping us all waiting. That did have some effect. He started and seemed to wake up, and then very quickly he scribbled about a couple of lines on his paper, and showed it up with the rest. As it was the last, or nearly the last, to come in, and as Sampson had a good deal to say to the boys who had written *meminiscimus patri meo* and the rest of it, it turned out that the clock struck twelve before he had got to McLeod, and McLeod had to wait afterwards to have his sentence corrected. There was nothing much going on outside when I got out, so I waited for him to come. He came very slowly when he did arrive, and I guessed there had been some sort of trouble. "Well," I said, "what did you get?" "Oh, I don't know," said McLeod, "nothing much: but I think Sampson's rather sick with me."'

'"Why, did you show him up some rot?" "No fear," he said. "It was all right as far as I could see: it was like this: *Memento* that's right enough for remember, and it takes a genitive *memento putei inter quatuor taxos*." "What silly rot!" I said. "What made you shove that down? What does it mean?" "That's the funny part," said McLeod. "I'm not quite sure what it does mean. All I know is, it just came into my head and I corked it down. I know what I think it means, because just before I wrote it down I had a sort of picture of it in my head: I believe it means 'Remember the well among the four' what are those dark sort of trees that have red berries on them?" "Mountain ashes, I s'pose you mean." "I never heard of them," said McLeod; "no, I'll tell you, yews."'

'"Well, and what did Sampson say?" "Why, he was jolly odd about it. When he read it he got up and went to the mantelpiece and stopped quite a long time without saying anything, with his back to me. And then he said, without turning round, and rather quiet, "What do you suppose that means?" I told him what I thought; only I couldn't remember the name of the silly tree: and then he wanted to know why I put it down, and I had to say something or other. And after that he left off talking about it, and asked me how long I'd been here, and where my people lived, and things like that: and then I came away: but he wasn't looking a bit well.'

'I don't remember any more that was said by either of us about this. Next day McLeod took to his bed with a chill or something of the kind, and it was a week or more before he was in school again. And as much as a month went by without anything happening that was noticeable. Whether or not Mr Sampson was really startled, as McLeod had thought, he didn't show it. I am pretty sure, of course, now, that there was something very curious in his past history, but I'm not going to pretend that we boys were sharp enough to guess any such thing.'

'There was one other incident of the same kind as the last which I told you. Several times since that day we had had to make up examples in school to illustrate different rules, but there had never been any row except when we did them wrong. At last there came a day when we were going through those dismal things which people call Conditional Sentences, and we were told to make a conditional sentence, expressing a future consequence. We did it, right or wrong, and showed up our bits of paper, and Sampson began looking through them. All at once he got up, made some odd sort of noise in his throat, and rushed out by a door that was just by his desk. We sat there for a minute or two, and then I suppose it was incorrect but we went up, I and one or two others, to look at the papers on his desk. Of course I thought someone must have put down some nonsense or other, and Sampson had gone off to report him. All the same, I noticed that he hadn't taken any of the papers with him when he ran out. Well, the top paper on the desk was written in red ink—which no one used and it wasn't in anyone's hand who was in the class. They all looked at it, McLeod and all, and took their dying oaths that it wasn't theirs. Then I thought of counting the bits of paper. And of this I made quite certain: that there were seventeen bits of paper on the desk, and sixteen boys in the form. Well, I bagged the extra paper, and kept it, and I believe I have it now. And now you will want to know what was written on it. It was simple enough, and harmless enough, I should have said.'

'"*Si tu non veneris ad me, ego veniam ad te,*" which means, I suppose, "If you don't come to me, I'll come to you."'

'Could you show me the paper?' interrupted the listener.

'Yes, I could: but there's another odd thing about it. That same afternoon I took it out of my locker I know for certain it was the same bit, for I made a finger-mark on it and no single trace of writing of any kind was there on it. I kept it, as I said, and since that time I have tried various experiments to see whether sympathetic ink had been used, but absolutely without result.'

'So much for that. After about half an hour Sampson looked in again: said he had felt very unwell, and told us we might go. He came rather gingerly to his desk and gave just one look at the uppermost paper: and I suppose he thought he must have been dreaming: anyhow, he asked no questions.'

'That day was a half-holiday, and next day Sampson was in school again, much as usual. That night the third and last incident in my story happened.'

'We, McLeod and I, slept in a dormitory at right angles to the main building. Sampson slept in the main building on the first floor. There was a very bright full moon. At an hour which I can't tell exactly, but some time between one and two,

I was woken up by somebody shaking me. It was McLeod; and a nice state of mind he seemed to be in. "Come," he said, "come! There's a burglar getting in through Sampson's window." As soon as I could speak, I said, "Well, why not call out and wake everybody up?" "No, no," he said, "I'm not sure who it is: don't make a row: come and look." Naturally I came and looked, and naturally there was no one there. I was cross enough, and should have called McLeod plenty of names: only I couldn't tell why it seemed to me that there was something wrong something that made me very glad I wasn't alone to face it. We were still at the window looking out, and as soon as I could, I asked him what he had heard or seen. "I didn't hear anything at all," he said, "but about five minutes before I woke you, I found myself looking out of this window here, and there was a man sitting or kneeling on Sampson's window-sill, and looking in, and I thought he was beckoning." "What sort of man?" McLeod wriggled. "I don't know," he said, "but I can tell you one thing he was beastly thin: and he looked as if he was wet all over: and," he said, looking round and whispering as if he hardly liked to hear himself, "I'm not at all sure that he was alive."'

'We went on talking in whispers some time longer, and eventually crept back to bed. No one else in the room woke or stirred the whole time. I believe we did sleep a bit afterwards, but we were very cheap next day.'

'And next day Mr Sampson was gone: not to be found: and I believe no trace of him has ever come to light since. In thinking it over, one of the oddest things about it all has seemed to me to be the fact that neither McLeod nor I ever mentioned what we had seen to any third person whatever. Of course no

questions were asked on the subject, and if they had been, I am inclined to believe that we could not have made any answer: we seemed unable to speak about it.'

'That is my story,' said the narrator. 'The only approach to a ghost story connected with a school that I know, but still, I think, an approach to such a thing.'

***

The sequel to this may perhaps be reckoned highly conventional; but a sequel there is, and so it must be produced. There had been more than one listener to the story, and, in the latter part of that same year, or of the next, one such listener was staying at a country house in Ireland.

One evening his host was turning over a drawer full of odds and ends in the smoking-room. Suddenly he put his hand upon a little box. 'Now,' he said, 'you know about old things; tell me what that is.' My friend opened the little box, and found in it a thin gold chain with an object attached to it. He glanced at the object and then took off his spectacles to examine it more narrowly. 'What's the history of this?' he asked. 'Odd enough,' was the answer. 'You know the yew thicket in the shrubbery: well, a year or two back we were cleaning out the old well that used to be in the clearing here, and what do you suppose we found?'

'Is it possible that you found a body?' said the visitor, with an odd feeling of nervousness.

'We did that: but what's more, in every sense of the word, we found two.'

'Good Heavens! Two? Was there anything to show how they got there? Was this thing found with them?'

'It was. Amongst the rags of the clothes that were on one

of the bodies. A bad business, whatever the story of it may have been. One body had the arms tight round the other. They must have been there thirty years or more—long enough before we came to this place. You may judge we filled the well up fast enough. Do you make anything of what's cut on that gold coin you have there?'

'I think I can,' said my friend, holding it to the light (but he read it without much difficulty); 'it seems to be GWS, July 24, 1865.'

THE DARE OF DEATH

Adil Marawala

The falling rays of the sun cast a golden mist in the evening sky at Giza. As the last flock of tourists gathered to watch a sound and light show retired from the comforts of cushioned seating to a humpback ride back to the hotel, the daylong crowded narrow lanes now became a private walkway for young Naseer, heading back home from his evening Quran classes. Naseer glanced through the headlines of *Al Khuit,* the local evening newspaper. His eyes followed the faint light from flickering lanterns along the road to read:

'Camel Fair attracts tourists'

'Total Lunar Eclipse Tonight'

'Dry winds on the rise; Khamsin may hit Giza'

The Camel Fair—that reminded Naseer that his cousin, Nisaar, was going to come tonight. Nisaar, a year or two older than Naseer, would travel with his parents on a nomadic trip across the Sahara desert rearing, training and trading the finest breeds of camels in Egypt. At his age, Nisaar was doing the rungs of camel training himself—he could saddle and ride the camel, round up a bunch of runaway camels, give the young camels a bath and even brand the new ones. Nisaar's father would allow him to lead the colourful decorated camel pack at the fair and even participate in the fierce camel race starting from the Giza football ground and ending at the foot of the Pyramids. His grandmother said Nisaar could join the Royal Egyptian Guards someday.

The Lunar Eclipse—no wonder the streets were vacant today. Naseer took the same route home every day and was used to seeing men huddled up on carpets bragging about their best trade of the day, their biggest catch of fish, their moments of mischief with a belly dancer or their triumph at duping a tourist and getting more money for their wares by promoting them as antiques. The roadside eateries, sizzling with smoked meat kababs, oven fresh bread, spicy liver gravy rolled in *shwarma* and the queue of people waiting for a glass of rose milk to bring relief to their burning tongues, were absent. Watching a lunar eclipse or letting the shadow of an eclipse fall on you is thought to bring bad luck for seven generations. Naseer had heard his grandmother say that the shadow of the eclipse can fill your heart with the darkness of death and the person would be reduced to dust before the rise of the new moon. Naseer raised his cap-covered head to watch the moon, the eclipse hadn't started yet ... and he had better hurry home.

The Khamsin—the violent dust storms that rise from the hot Sahara desert fill the air with waves of sand and cast a murky cloud, blanketing the sunlight. Naseer had read that once when the French Army, under the command of General Napolean Bonaparte, decided to invade Egypt, the deadly Khamsin arose from the east of Giza. The natives went to take cover, while the French did not react until it was too late, then choked and fainted in the blinding, suffocating walls of dust. Grains of sand whirled by the wind blinded the soldiers and created electrical disturbances that rendered compasses useless. His grandmother, in many of her story-tellings, had pictured the Khamsin as the army of Anubis, the God of Death, riding towards the Home of the Damned—resting ground of the dead in the West. Anything caught in the Khamsin gets its soul sucked out of the body.

Violent storms or not, Naseer always experienced a cold draught whistle past his neck whenever he was walking alone in the night on his way home. He always felt he was being followed. Something was keeping an eye on him, it would rustle in the rosebush as he left the Quran class, whistle through the waterpipes and open sewers, ruffle the tents and curtains along the way. As the street narrowed down into a one-man passageway, the cold breeze would intensify and breathe on Naseer's ears, almost pinching him at the back of his neck. At times Naseer would run the distance of the narrow passageway leading to his home but the cold feeling wouldn't leave him, sinking its teeth into his skin as if it were a leech sucking the warmth of life out of him. It would only take the presence of his mother at the doorstep to shake off the scary chill and make Naseer take a deep breath of relief.

Naseer ran the last home stretch at a frantic pace today, not only to beat the chill but also the eclipse. However, instead of his mother, he saw Nisaar open the door and let him in.

'When did you come, Nisaar? Where are Ammi and Abba?'

'They have gone with my Ammi and Abba to a function in the City Palace. They said they will return in an hour or two, or after the eclipse ends. Get inside quickly, or the shadow of the moon will fall on you.'

Naseer rushed in, greeting his brother with a smile, dropped his Arabic notebooks on the floor, washed his face and returned with the duo's favourite pastime—Snakes and Ladders.

'Let's get the rules straight. You climb a ladder or go down the snake only when you land on the square. You win only if you land on the final square with the right moves. You can escape going down the snake only once in the game by doing a dare.' Naseer plugged all the loopholes from which Nisaar could sneak out a win.

'You are learning from the past ... good to see that, brother. Lets play.'

The dice kept rolling and the two brothers tried to out race each other on the board. While jostling for lead halfway in the game, Naseer spotted a glowing button on Nisaar's coat.

'What's that, Nisaar?'

'Oh, that is a gold medal I got today for being the youngest camel rider in the main race. It has an eagle's symbol imprinted on a gold coin. I feel this will bring me luck.'

And sure enough, Nisaar was rolling a straight series of sixes on the dice and was soon ahead of Naseer. He had always been ahead of Naseer. At times this used to irk Naseer. But he was proud of his brother's achievements and was not one to give a fight away without throwing a punch. Naseer, too, rolled out some heavy numbers and was soon running neck to neck with Nisaar.

Just then a rumble in the skies followed by a gust of wind interrupted their game. The Khamsin was approaching, windows began rattling and curtains assumed ghoulish forms and waved about. Naseer was reminded of the chilly winds that haunted him every day. He moved towards the windows and attempted to close them.

'Nisaar, help me bolt the windows!' cried Naseer.

'Oh, come on. Use your strength, do it yourself … you are a big boy now.'

Naseer gave all the power he had and tried pulling the windows towards himself. He looked up at the night sky. For a moment he was entranced by the advancing shadow engulfing the moon. Was it a bad thing to do? Should he continue looking at nature's marvel or retreat before it filled him with darkness …

With great effort Naseer put a latch on the windows and shaking the dust off his clothes, came back to resume the game.

'Hey! What's this, Nisaar? My rook was on 45 and not 35. Did you move it?'

'You must be dreaming. The last time you played it was on 35.'

'Don't cheat, Nisaar, I was only five places behind you.'

'Oh, stop crying like a baby. If you want to win put your piece anywhere you want and still I will beat you. You should be more careful of noting your position.'

'I don't cheat, Nisaar. I just rose to lock the windows because the Khamsin is coming.'

'So what, are you scared of the Khamsin? Look at you … a grown up boy and still scared of a harmless wind.'

'It is not harmless, it can fill your lungs with dust and choke you to death. Grandmother said …'

'Oh forget about grandmother, I have faced the Khamsin head on with my father when we took the caravan of camels across the Sahara. And nothing happened to me.'

'You are not scared of the Khamsin? Have you ever felt like the wind is trying to catch you from behind and sink its cold teeth into your body?'

'Rubbish. We are brave people and fearless. You sound like a scared sissy girl.'

'But, brother, the Khamsin is said to be the wind of evil spirits. Don't you do something to protect yourself?'

'You sound like a coward, Naseer! Why should we be afraid of nature? A few years ago, when an old chief was guiding the nomads, he used to sacrifice a baby camel by letting the animal go astray in the Khamsin and hope the evil spirits would follow him and move away from the caravan. But when my father took charge, he abolished the practice. Many people cautioned him, saying it will bring bad luck to his family, but he did not listen. And nothing has happened to us, in fact we are getting more price for our camels and, see, I won a medal today. Now lets get back to the game.'

'I am not afraid to lose … I am just …' Naseer stopped halfway. He did not want to admit he was scared of some strange things around him. Certainly not to Nisaar, who would then tease him.

'Tell you what, little brother, you can hop on back to position 45, if you do a dare.'

Naseer knew Nisaar had found his weakness and was ready to mock him. But a jump of ten points seemed crucial to him. Nisaar's pep talk of being from a brave tribe had filled Naseer with a new found gusto and he felt ready to take on Nisaar's challenge.

'What's the dare?' Naseer asked.

'You have to spend two minutes in the dark basement, all by yourself.'

The dark basement was one of Naseer's worst nightmares. The place was damp, cold and quivering with weird noises—squeaking rats, possibly hissing cobras and scorpions clicking their pincers. Just the thought of entering the basement gave him the shivers. But he was committed to proving a point to Nisaar. He, too, wanted to be seen as a brave boy.

'I'll do it. But on one condition. When I come out of the basement, you will give me your gold medal,' Naseer tried one last trick to make Nisaar change his mind.

'Done! You can have my medal,' came Nisaar's reply. Naseer prepared to face his worst fears.

The moment Naseer took two steps down the ramp leading to the basement below, Nisaar shut the door with a loud thud. Naseer thought he would be considerate enough to wait for him to walk down the ramp, but no.

As Naseer took one small step at a time he removed his slippers so as not to make squeaky sounds which would invite a cobra to mistake his foot for a morsel of rat meat. He took small breaths so as not to wake up any bat sleeping upside down in the wooden columns. On his way down, he missed a step and tumbled all the way, landing on a sack of dry firewood. The wood was tied with a rope. Naseer waved his hands around to get a feel of the place. His hands touched the rope and he mistook it for a snake. Naseer gave out a loud shriek. He was almost in tears. He couldn't see anything in the dark basement. He could smell the dampness and hear the hearty laugh Nisaar was having at his expense.

'The two minutes are over, Nisaar, let me out!'

'Why not stay for a few more minutes inside? You wanted my gold medal, right? It won't come to you that easily.'

He fumbled around in the dark till he spotted a streak of light peering through the basement wall. He moved closer to the light and huddled around it. The light was of the moon in the night sky, now almost overcast by the shadow of the eclipse. Just as the moon was fully eclipsed, Naseer felt a cold sensation run down his spine. Was the cold air an evil spirit? Had the eclipse made it stronger? Would it kill him in the basement? Naseer fought off all the tricks his mind was playing on him and slowly began to climb up the ramp towards the basement door. He banged on the doors with all his might and cried, 'Nisaar, please let me out ! I don't feel good in here!'

'But I am feeling good seeing you scared … Ha ha ha,' Nisaar laughed back.

'That's not funny. Let me out!'

Nisaar finally unlocked the door and Naseer threw himself on the floor, gasping for breath. He picked up his cap, looked at Nisaar rolling on the floor, and retreated to the washroom to clean his face.

When he came back, Nisaar had laid down another game for him.

'Welcome to the light, my brother. I have kept my word, Here's your gamepiece on position 45. As for the medal, I think you are too scared a person to deserve this. Still I am willing to give it to you provided you beat me in Snakes and Ladders.'

One look at the board game and Naseer understood the ploy.

29

'Oh, Nisaar. I should have known you would not change from your cheating ways. You have kept me on 45 but placed your piece on 95.'

'And I am one roll of dice away from winning. Nothing can stop me now ...' Nisaar shouted in triumph and rolled his final call.

The dice, as luck would have it, had other ideas. Nisaar got 3 points which landed him on 98, the box bearing the longest serpent of the game, threatening to drag Nisaar down to number 2.

'Damn the snake,' mumbled Nisaar.

'It doesn't pay to cheat, Nisaar,' said Naseer.

'Hold on, wise guy. I still have the power of a dare left. Dare me anything you will and I will do it.'

Naseer stopped to think. Nisaar could take on all challenges with ease. He was a champion camel rider, a rough and tough boy soon to get into the Royal Army. What could possibly knock the wind out of his sails?

While Naseer's mind searched for a suitable dare, his senses seemed to guide him to an answer. He could smell the dryness of air outside. He looked out of the glass windows to see the moon rising out of the demonic shadows. His mind was made up.

'I dare you to face the Khamsin for two minutes.'

'Are you kidding? The Khamsin is at its peak outside and you want me to go out?'

'Why are you afraid? Haven't you faced the Khamsin before?'

'I have, but not alone. I was there with Abba by my side.'

'Well ... a dare is a dare. Either you honour it or you slide down the snake, lose the game and hand me your medal.'

'Never,' replied Nisaar, and placed the medal on the game board.

'I will face the Khamsin. But only for two minutes.'

'Nothing less and nothing more. I honour my word, unlike some people I know.'

'Alright. It's a deal.' Nisaar put on his coat and slowly opened the door. A wave of dust slapped his face. He took a deep breath and plunged out.

Naseer felt bad and wondered if it was right to let Nisaar out in the Khamsin. But the humiliation he had suffered a few minutes ago was still fresh and made him think whatever he was doing was right. He could hear the voices outside. The windows were being battered by the dust storms.

Suddenly a loud shriek filled the room. Naseer was quick to realise Nisaar was in discomfort. He tried opening the door. But the winds were too strong for him. He rubbed the glass eyepatch on the door to take a peek outside. Nisaar was nowhere to be seen. Naseer was scared. He pulled the door open with all his might. The Khamsin was throwing dunes of dust in all directions. There was no trace of human life. Nisaar was nowhere to be seen. Before Naseer could react or shout for Nisaar, a huge gust of dust-laden wind hit him in the face and slammed the door shut. Naseer was out in the midst of the Khamsin. He could feel the sand enter his nostrils. He kept his face to the ground and covered it with his cap as if wearing a gas mask. The blows of wind soon knocked him unconscious. It took the comforting hand of his mother to wake up Naseer. At first he couldn't remember anything but soon arose from the bed and asked, 'Nisaar … where is he?'

His father replied, 'Nisaar! Had he come here? Strange, because he did not come till we had left for the palace. He was supposed to receive a medal at the palace yesterday night but he did not arrive there as well.'

'No! He was here. I played ... he dared me ... we ... then I ...'

Naseer was at a loss for words to explain what had happened that night. He looked at the gameboard lying on the floor. He reached down to find a gold medal of an eagle inscribed on a gold coin.

The medal was pinned to the morning paper, whose headlines read:

'Khamsin winds blow across Giza'

'Camel Traders leave Giza fairgrounds overnight'

'Body of a young boy found buried in the west. Nature of death unknown.'

THE SHADOW PEOPLE

Meenakshi Reddy Madhavan

hen Yamini stepped out at Vilasgunj station, she was surprised to see that there was no one there. Even for a small town—well, perhaps, *because* it was a small town—Vilasgunj had a surprisingly busy station. There was a magazine man and an oranges woman and usually Anant Ram, the old, wizened station master, who knew everybody. But today it seemed abandoned and all Yamini could see were the twisting shadows from the trees. She was even more surprised that for the first time in her life, nobody had come to receive her. It was her first day back from boarding school, it was the *holidays*, and she had a trunk and couldn't be expected to carry it all the way home. Well, at least she thought she had a trunk.

Yamini watched in astonishment as the train pulled out of the station leaving absolutely nothing behind. 'Hey!' she yelled, running after it, 'hey! My trunk!' Nope. There was no indication of the train stopping or even anyone listening to her. This was a very bad day, and Yamini set her teeth, preparing to go home and complain to her mother. Then she would be fed mangoes, and she would play with the dogs and maybe in the evening, go swimming with her cousins. Nothing was so bad that it ruined the summer holidays. It was probably a mix up, she said to herself comfortingly. They probably expect me tomorrow, and how surprised they'll be to see me walk in and everyone will feel really bad for me. She smiled to herself at the thought of the adults' aghast faces. She could milk this for a while.

The fact that ghosts come out at night is a myth, just like many other things in this world. They still retain some of their human traits and like to sleep like the rest of us. There are scary things that appear in the middle of the night—monsters and werewolves and things wanting revenge—but, god preserve us, not ghosts.

Maybe she could get a lift along the way, thought Yamini. Having lived her entire life in Vilasgunj at 'Chaudhury ka bungalow' people knew her and her family. She was confident that anyone seeing her trudging along in the heat would stop and offer to drop her home. The bungalow was about two kilometres away and her shoes hurt as the sun beat down on her hair. But the rest of the town was as empty as the station. Was it a festival day? Sometimes people retired to their houses on special occasions, spending time with their families till the evening when they made house calls and distributed sweets. Her family was quite involved with all town happenings, and if it *was* a festival day, then that would explain why they had forgotten to pick her up. Yamini tried not to get too frustrated with the heat and her

shoes and her confusion. It would be better soon. She just
wanted her mother.

Walking home, Yamini felt somehow like she was in a
dream. Not a good dream, or even necessarily, a nightmare, just
one of those dreams where you float around and everything
seems sort of surreal. She put it down to the baking heat, and
felt her forehead to see if she was getting a fever. That gesture
once again reminded her of her mother, oh, how surprised
they'd all be when she got home, maybe she'd be put to bed,
with the AC roaring and someone to check in on her, feed her
mangoes from a plate. She didn't feel warm though, despite
the sun, she felt cool, as though she had been indoors all day.

*Most ghosts are pretty angry that there is no heaven. There is no
hell either, but no one* really *thinks they're going to hell. Instead they
are locked to earth, as much as they were when they were alive and
there's nowhere else for them to go.*

Yamini finally reached the large bungalow where her
family lived. She had described it to a school friend earlier
that term as, 'the biggest house in the town'. This was not
technically true. Yamini's house was not the biggest, but it had
the largest spread. Most houses were built vertically, four or
five storeys, in a concession to modernity, but hers sprawled
around a courtyard with a well, and each of the four walls
surrounding the courtyard had rooms that served different
purposes. Yamini's family lived in the side that faced west and
she could watch the sunset every evening from her room. When
she had been younger, she asked her mother why sunsets had
to happen. 'I want the day to go on and on,' she had said, her
face mutinous. Her mother had laughed, a little sadly, and said,
'The sun has to go spend time with other people now, baby.'

Later, her father had pulled out his old globe and demonstrated to her how the earth moved and how the sun shifted locations, but she had liked her mother's explanation better. Maybe they had gone to spend time with other people, too. Maybe they had forgotten all about her.

The old gate creaked as she pushed through it and with one last burst of energy she ran inside the house. 'Ma? Papa? I'm home!' she yelled as she ran from room to room. 'Chutki?' she called for her little sister, 'It's me, Yamini!' The house was empty, abandoned, but it didn't feel abandoned. It felt as though they had just stepped out for a moment and would be back soon. The cows mooed from the cow shed at her voice and she ran there to look for her father, her uncle, anyone. But there was no one there. The house waited quietly. In a burst of tears, Yamini ran into her room and wept.

Trouble maker ghosts are the origins of all ghost stories. Your grandmother wouldn't come back to haunt you. Sure, she watches you every now and then, but, then, like a soap opera you've given up on, you lose track of characters and then you just stop caring.

Yamini had fallen asleep crying and when she woke up, the sun had already set and she heard some faint murmurs from the rest of the house. Thinking it was her family back again, she got up a little groggily, and made her way outside. The house was dark, no lights on, but she could feel the closeness of people. She tried to switch on a light, but it didn't work. Yamini was a brave girl, used to frequent power cuts and not afraid of very much, having grown up with very sensible parents who reasoned her out of any imaginary frights, and many boy cousins who had tried pranks on her and failed. No electricity? Just light a candle, which she did, and began to move to the northward set of rooms. That was where the kitchen was and the dining room, and where the family gathered at the end of the day. The murmurs grew as she approached the dining room, but when she threw open the door, once more it was empty.

Or was it?

In front of Yamini's eyes, she watched her shadow leap in the candlelight and then she saw four or five other shadows joining it. There *were* people in this room. The wind murmured low in the trees outside, but perhaps it wasn't the wind. It was whispering noises, noises that made no sense when you confronted them, but if you closed your eyes, noises that were conversations. She gripped tightly onto her candle holder, watching as the shadows moved independently. One of the shadows noticed her, and before she could make a sound, grabbed on to her shadow and dragged it into the courtyard. And this time, *Yamini* was the shadow. She was forced to go along with her dark image, dragged as if they were sewn together at the feet, her hands shook and she dropped the candle, and she looked down and felt her body grow weirdly. It was as if she was looking into one of those 'fun' mirrors, she morphed into a creature with long flapping arms, her shoulder and torso grew very tall and her legs fused together so she couldn't walk.

But she didn't need to walk anymore, she was being pulled by her shadow into the courtyard and there around the well, she finally saw people. Dev, a second cousin who had drowned in this very well, Ayah who died when Yamini was about ten and who had worked for the family since Yamini's mother was a little girl, Dada, her grandfather who she had never met, but whose picture hung in the kitchen. For the first time in her life, Yamini felt a little flicker of fear.

These were … *go on, say i* … but it was impossible … *not impossible if you can see them* … these were … *dead people.*

The dead people around the well turned to her and smiled, and Ayah, who was the one who had grabbed Yamini's shadow, let it go. Yamini watched as it bounced towards her and then gasped as it bounced into her. Her legs separated, then fused, then separated again. Her stomach clenched and she thought she was going to vomit, and then her body shrank massively and she was thrown to the ground. When she stood up a little dazed, she looked down and noticed she could see the grass and the stones and the moonlight shine through her body. She was flat, uni-dimensional. She was, in short, her shadow.

'Why are you here?' she squeaked, 'Where is my family? What has happened to me?'

'Dear Yamini,' said Dada, his own shadow self flickering by the well. 'Your family is well. They're inside.'

'No, they're not!' she screamed. 'They're not, they're not, they're *not*! What have you done with them?'

'Yamini, beta,' Ayah stepped towards her. 'You're a shadow person now.'

'But I don't *want* to be a shadow person! Let me go!'

'Go then,' said Dev, smiling. 'Go run inside and find your mummy-daddy and they'll tell you this is all a dream. Go on!'

'Dev!' said Dada, sternly.

'What? If she wants to go, send her. I have other things to do than sit around and listen to her scream.'

'Dev, it's not easy for anyone,' said Ayah.

'Well,' said Dev, still looking annoyed, 'I've been a Shadow Person longer than you have, and frankly, I'm a little bored of having to go over the explanations over and over again.'

Yamini didn't stop to hear anymore. She raced through her house, going, 'Ma! Mumma! Please come out!' until she had been everywhere and they were nowhere and once more she was facing the three ghosts.

'*Not* ghosts,' said Dada. '*Shadow* people.'

Yamini went over to a bench and sat down. If ghost was the same as a shadow person, if they had called her a shadow person, it meant that … 'Am I a ghost?' she asked.

'Shadow person!' said Dev, looking crosser.

'Ayah?' said Yamini, her lower lip beginning to quiver.

'Darling girl,' said Ayah, her wonderful comforting face making Yamini feel much better, 'We are all shadow people. Even your parents.'

Wild hope leaped up in Yamini. 'Can I see *them*?' she asked. Dev laughed mockingly and Dada made his form stretch till it reached the top floor. 'Dev! One more peep out of you, and I will have you banished from the grounds for fifty years.'

'Not like I want to stay anyway,' muttered Dev, but he shut up.

'There are two kinds of shadow people,' said Dada.

'The ones who breathe and the ones who don't. We can only see each other. The breathers can only see each other also. Once in a great while, a non breather and breather will be able to meet, but these instances are rare.'

'But I breathe,' said Yamini.

Ayah's eyes were kind as they rested on her face. 'Try,' she said.

Yamini realised she had been holding her breath this entire time, and oddly, she didn't feel the funny bursting feeling she normally did. She exhaled and inhaled and then began to cough. She only regained herself once she took in a mouthful of air and held her breath. It felt, weirdly, natural.

'What does this mean?' she asked, and then she knew.

'Am I dead?'

'*Finally!*' said Dev, 'I thought you were going to take forever, and we aren't allowed to tell you, you have to figure it out for yourself. Yes, you're dead, you died on your way to catch a train back home. Run over by a bus.' He made a flattening motion with his hand. 'Shmush. Dead. Like roadkill.'

Dada's eyes flashed and Dev shrunk, suddenly half his size.

'She had to know!' he squeaked.

Yamini thought back. Funnily, she couldn't remember getting on the train, or even the journey. She had assumed she had slept the whole way, but she would have surely had *some* memory of it.

'There is no heaven,' Ayah began and the other two joined in, speaking low, like they were chanting:

There is no heaven, there is no hell. The world is what it is.
Breathers hear us, we hear breathers, but we can never meet.
Shadows live, under breather's feet, until the breather is no more.
Shadows wait, dancing in the light, to take you where they were.
Then shadow and breather combine, and we are one.
We are Shadow People.

The hair on Yamini's arms stood straight up. The courtyard was flooded with light and shadows. The whispers came back. *We are Shadow People*, said the trees and the wind. *We are Shadow*

People, murmured the other figures, suddenly everywhere. I am dead, thought Yamini, and her body began to glow in the moonlight, I am dead and I am a shadow person.

It's funny how nothing seemed to matter anymore. Not the ghosts of wails she could hear from inside the house or the year—or was it a hundred—that passed her by.

THEN THERE WAS ONE

Jane De Suza

fist punching my shoulder woke me up. 'Hey Sissy, let's see how brave you are. We're going into the hill tunnel. Get out of bed.' My watch showed one in the morning and the tent was pitch black inside except for the face of my tormentor, Raghu, ghostly in the green light of my watch, shaking me awake.

Okay, some background first, I guess. I am eleven, thin and, you know, the non-sporty kind. The thickest thing about me is my glasses. Obviously then, my folks, in some misguided attempt to toughen me up, sent me to this week-long adventure camp. Almost at once, I became the favourite punching bag of a rough gang of 14-year-old hulks: Akhil with biceps like logs, Sam who was built like a truck, and Raghu, who was the worst kind of nasty, who'd pin a butterfly's wings down.

The camp put us through some cliff-climbing, rapelling and

that sort of stuff. We had set up tents in a forest clearing; and on one trek, when we got kind of lost on a hill, we had stumbled upon an old wooden door, hidden by long grass, in the hillside rock. The locals never went near it—it led to some unholy stuff, they said. They left little pots of sweets or garlands outside the door to appease whichever angry demonic force lived within.

On the last night of camp, when Raghu woke me up, I was so exhausted and so happy to be going home, I didn't fight it anymore. 'Okay,' I said, 'I'm not scared. Let's go'. I'd prove to them that I was no baby.

So, on that moonless night, the four of us picked our way across the brambles scratching our legs, up to the hill and to the hidden door. The others kept prodding me along. 'Hey Missy, got your night facecream on? You look pale.'

We found the small door and tried to push it open. No. Sam put his huge shoulder against it. No. We all began to kick it then, till, with a blood-curdling whine, it creaked open. We looked at each other. No one had really expected it to open. It was tar-black inside.

'Go in first, Sissy!' Raghu hissed. I looked around, worried, but the three mocking faces, with eyes glinting, made my mind up for me. So I got onto my knees and crawled in. The tunnel was only about the height of a small boy, and so we had to crouch. I heard the others following me. We had no torches, except for the light out of our watches.

Wham! We screamed because it was just so sudden, yes, all four of us. Swivelling around, we saw that the hillside door had shut. Akhil, who was last, moved over to it and tried to open it. We all pushed. It wouldn't budge at all. We pulled and kicked, then with a knot in our stomachs, decided to just move on. Maybe the tunnel would lead out of another door?

That's when we first heard it. A faraway lonely horn, the sort that an old trumpet or wind pipe would make. 1- 2 - 3 - 4. Four blasts of a rusty old horn coming from somewhere deep within the hillside. But it couldn't be 4 o'clock. It had been barely half an hour since we'd left. What was that horn counting?

The tunnel sloped upwards sharply, and so we were out of breath in a few minutes. In the dark, lit up by eerie green watch lights, gasping along, I felt something brush against my face. 'No!' I gasped. Was it a bat? A moth? Or that supposed hill demon? The others tried to laugh, piteously, frightened themselves.

Another gasp. This time it wasn't me. It came from the back of our troop. Akhil stuttered, 'No. No. Oh please no!'

'What is it, dude?' We turned around trying to focus our watch lights on him. Had he fallen and injured himself?

Weird! Where was he? There was just no Akhil. There was only a frightened Raghu behind me, and a shivering Sam. No Akhil at the rear.

'Akhil!' we called out. No answer. We tried to train our watch lights on the walls—a hidden side-tunnel maybe. Nothing.

Then the horn began to blow slowly and sadly again. 1 - 2 - 3.

'It's counting us,' I whispered. 'That horn blew four times for four of us. Now, it's blowing only thrice.'

Our hearts were beating so loudly, we could probably hear each other's. Raghu pushed me and sent me sprawling forward.

'Go! Go you little idiot! Move it! Move on! Run!'

My knee had cut from the fall, and I could feel warm blood dripping down my leg. Oh god, let there be no blood-sucking beast in here which would nose me out. My eyes fogged up behind my glasses and I pushed my way upwards. My legs were aching and my ribcage throbbing but I pushed on.

Raghu hissed. 'Let's put the scaredy-poo at the back, Sam. Let him get picked off next by whatever demon this is.'

I scrambled up the tunnel rockface desperately. Raghu's hand shot out and tried to grab my ankle, but I kicked out frantically.

'Ow!' Raghu called out. 'You little creep. I'll get you. I'll wring your neck, I'll …'

A loud cackle cut into his threats. The tunnel began to echo with eerie cackling—a rusty old laugh that went on and on. The hollow tunnel reverberated with it, multiplying it many times over till it surrounded us.

I sobbed, and tried to pull myself on. I'd read a lot of books. I could name about a dozen different evil spirits, but they were not real. Not real, I tried to remind myself. They were just imaginary—imagined up by writers the world over. There was no demonic force. I would win this race just on my intellect—I had more brains than those bullies behind me combined. There. Was. No. Evil. Force. I told myself. But then—where did Akhil disappear? What was that horn? What was that cackling?

Another brush of something across my cheek, followed by a cackling laugh again. All three of us screamed, and the screams joined the echoing laughter.

When the noise finally stopped, and all that was audible was our sobbing, we pushed onwards and upwards with a sudden frantic energy we didn't even know we had. I forgot the pain of cut knees, bruised knuckles, and just climbed up, over rocky, wet, slimy rockface in that dark tunnel.

We pushed on, sobbing, praying, whispering that we'd never do anything like this again. No playing hookie. No …

'My watch light's gone,' whispered Sam. 'Raghu, will you stop pulling at my neck!'

Raghu replied. 'I'm not. I'm ahead of you.'

Sam said in a gush of words, 'Then who is dragging me by my neck? Who's behind me? Akhil—is that you? Oh my god, what is that? What …'

His voice just stopped abruptly. Raghu and I swung backwards to see nothing. Sam, blubbering and sobbing, had quietened down. We couldn't hear him anymore, and couldn't see him either.

I gulped. This could not be happening.

But it was! The horn began to blow mournfully. 1 - 2. Just two.

'Raghu, pinch me. It's a dream. I'm going home tomorrow,' I cried. I was just a little boy and I wanted to go home to my folks, to my little sister, to my books. I wanted to wake up from this nightmare.

Raghu lunged at me and pinched my ear hard. He twisted it around too, till I yelled.

'Is that enough for you, Sissy?' he whispered angrily. 'You think this is some game, you idiot? Something out of your fairy tale books?'

I found some inner core of steel I didn't even know I had and pulled myself upwards again. Climbing up, my hands reaching out to the rock and pulling myself upwards, gasping, awash in sweat.

Raghu gasped behind me. 'Wait, you idiot. Don't you dare try to get away from me. I'm not going to die in this place. It's you next!'

He reached out and grabbed at my leg and I tried to shake him off, kick him off, but he'd caught on this time. I felt his fingers wrap around my ankle. 'No!' I cried. 'Don't, please!'

Raghu pulled himself up so that we were both at the same level in that upward sloping tunnel. He grabbed my upper arm, and hissed, 'You go to the back.'

'No. Raghu, listen. We're the only two left. This demon is taking whoever is at the back. And then one of us will be alone.' I cried, frantically trying to find some way to get out of this on my brainpower, to save us, to save myself. 'Look, if we both stick together, there won't be any one at the back or front. This evil thing can't pick us out if we're both together. No one at the back, okay?'

I could see from the fading light of Raghu's watch, since mine had faded away too, that he was trying to make up his mind.

The eerie laughter began again and that seemed to do it. Raghu gripped me, digging into the flesh of my arm. 'Okay, go! Let's try it your way. Together. Go!'

Together, we pushed up, forcing our way through strings of what was cold, misty, clammy water? Spider webs? Cutting our elbows and knees on the rock—pushing upwards, dreading the next pealing of the horn.

Why did we have to come in here? I wished I had just stayed in bed, and had not tried to prove anything. I thought of my little sister waiting for me to come home from camp and forced back another sob. I had to get out of this alive. I had to.

47

Somewhere deep down, I felt it was useless. The demonic forces of the hill were claiming their victims. We were their prey. We had invaded their privacy, their homes kept secret for probably centuries—and here we were, silly schoolboys stumbling upon ancient secrets. They would not let us go.

Raghu let out a yell. 'What the …! My foot!' He shouted in pain. 'My foot is caught!' We looked down, and his foot was lodged in some sort of hole in the ground. Oh my god, is this how the others had disappeared? Through some holes in the tunnel—into the hillside—to lie buried forever?

'Pull me out!' Raghu cried, and I stared at him. This was the guy who had made my week at camp a living hell. He had tormented me, bullied me, made me cry, made me look like a fool in front of everyone—so many times. I could leave him there and let the demon of the hill claim its next victim. I turned forward and upwards to leave. Then I stopped.

I couldn't.

All that was decent and good within me stopped me from moving ahead. I knew it was my only hope to go it alone, but I couldn't. I couldn't just leave him to die there.

Choking back a sob, because I knew it was back to the battle of the two of us again—I reached out my thin arms and grabbed him around the chest. He heaved and I heaved and with another yell, his foot pulled out.

Raghu was breathing heavily and crying openly. This big bully. If only the other boys at camp could see him now. 'I almost went, man, I almost died out there. You saved me, man.'

'It's okay, Raghu, let's just go on,' I said. 'Together, remember?'

Then over our sobs, came the long, sad, blood-curdling

blowing of the horn. Clearly. Once. Just one long siren. We waited for the next. For 2. Silence. There was just one. One of us would go.

We looked at each other terrified. A cold clammy hand of fear slid down my spine. This was it. One of us was going to be sacrificed now. Disappear forever. To appease the demons of the hill.

'It's not going to be me,' hissed Raghu, his eyes narrow and glinting in the fading green light of his watch, and he grabbed my shoulder and pushed me back—back into that hole into which he'd almost fallen.

'No, no, Raghu, no!' I screamed, but I was no match for his huge bulk. I felt myself falling and the last thing I saw above me was Raghu's face, evil glimmering out of his eyes. And it struck me—it wasn't just pure evil inside the hillside, there was evil hiding in each one of us; it's just that in many of us, the good won over the evil.

Everything was black. I fell, tumbling, rolling, my back and legs scraping against rock, screaming, praying, lower and lower, until I saw I was tumbling towards an orange light. A fire? Oh my god, this was the fire within the belly of the mountain. I was falling to my death—to the demon's cave? To their furnace?

You read in these circumstances how people black out, right? That would have been merciful. But I was conscious of every long drawn moment.

Finally, I fell out into that light, eyes shut out of sheer fear of what I would find myself in. I wasn't ready to confront the demons of the hillside, I was absolutely terrified. There was a lot of shouting and I steeled myself for whatever was coming next. Slowly I opened my eyes.

I was out on the hillside again, I had fallen right through the tunnel out of a hole in the hill. I found the camp coaches and other students and locals clustered around me with torches—that explained the light at the end of the tunnel. There was a search party out looking for us. I almost fainted in the arms of the coach.

In all the hushed silence, I heard the old voice of the local chief. 'This is the one that survived.'

I looked back at the hill and in my head, I heard the screaming, the cackling, the eerie laughter, the horn. Where had the others disappeared? Had they too escaped out of holes in the hillside, or had the hill demons claimed them?

***

A week later, when all the media excitement had died down, I held my little sister close to me on our verandah swing, while I went through the file of newspaper clippings about my 'miraculous' escape. The other three boys had never been found. And the door in the hillside had vanished. No one ever found it again.

THE BOOK

Samhita Arni

Many, many years ago, I chanced upon a strange, little bookshop in Old Town. It was a ramshackle operation, stacks of books lined the pavement, moulting pages in the noonday sun, arranged haphazardly—*The Communist Manifesto* keeping company with *The Wind in the Willows*, and Polidori's *Vampyre* lying precariously close to Austen's *Mansfield Park*, pages touching. I chuckled to myself, imagining what havoc was to unfold if Polidori's bloodsucking protagonist were to leap out of the covers and jump across pages, to sink his teeth into Lady Bertram's beloved Pug. Catastrophe would result, with a vampiric pug chasing down the corridors of Mansfield Park—turning all our beloved (and not so beloved) characters—Fanny, Edward, Henry Crawford, Ms Norris—into creatures of the night.

As I examined the contents of another pile, I stumbled

across a strange book. It was a tiny thing, with an ancient, black threadbare cover, leaves spilling out. I opened the book, and glanced across the first page. There was nothing—just a blank page. Puzzled, I flipped past pages until I came, in the middle of the book, to a white page, marred by a single black dot.

The dot grew, before my very eyes, it spread across the page and resolved itself into a picture, in the manner of a black and white etching.

It was a portrait of a young woman, who looked strangely familiar. As I looked at the picture, her features withered, her eyes grew rheumy, and lines etched themselves in the corner of her mouth. She was now, perhaps, in her late fifties, and even as I watched, the edges of the page began to burn and char, fire creeping slowly towards the center of the image. The woman looked at either side, at the burning edges that framed her, imprisoned her, and fear began to twist her features, furrow her brow. Her features melted into a pool of black ink, as her face began to burn, and her mouth opened in a soundless scream.

I shut the book.

The smell of burning still hung in the air, and my heart rocked in my chest. I shut my eyes, hoping to erase the image of her burning face, but it was still there, etched in darkness against my eyelids. I opened my eyes, shocked now, for I had realised why her features had been so familiar, why her face had tugged at my memory.

'Are you alright?' A voice sounded by my ear. I turned, it was a fellow customer, a sandy haired tourist, perusing the stacks of books on the pavement. I nodded and moved away, into the shop.

It was dark inside; it smelt of mothballs, dusty old pages and paan. I went to the cashier's desk, but there was only a little boy sleeping there, his head resting on a thick volume of Shakespeare.

'Is someone older here? Who owns this shop?' I asked, a little surprised. The boy shook his head, rubbing the sleep from his eyes.

'No, my grandfather is away, but you can pay here.' I sighed, I didn't imagine that this little boy would be much help in learning anything about the black book in my hands. 'When will your grandfather be back?' I asked.

The little boy shrugged, and then turning to a dark doorway behind him, shouted, 'Ammi!'

A woman answered, faintly, something I couldn't catch. As I waited, she emerged from the doorway, a pretty girl, I could tell, even in the darkness of the shop. She had almond shaped grey eyes, heavily lined with kohl, and a fair, smooth skin.

As she came in, she pulled her pink scarf over her hair, and her bangles jingled, a soft, sweet sound. She seemed very young, too young to have birthed the boy beside her. I was caught by her beauty, the beauty of an houri or a princess, a strange thing to find in the darkness of a bookshop.

The boy showed her the book. She frowned at the book, but didn't touch it, or glance at the pages. Smiling sweetly at me, she replied in beautiful, classical Urdu. 'I'm sorry, I can't help you. But my father will be back, next week, he's gone to his village.'

I bought the book, in any case, and left the shop. I opened it, many times in the following days, but it only ever showed me one picture, the picture I had already seen.

Months passed, and the book was lying, forgotten, in a drawer, when my nephew, a sweet six-year-old, came to stay with me. His parents, jet-setting executives, had little time to spend with their boy, and so he often came to me. He was a quiet, frail thing and we would work in comfortable silence together, he—industriously colouring little pictures of houses and families—and me, trying hard to transmute simple words and sentences into something much greater, into stories, plots and characters.

One day, though, the silence was broken by a little cry. I turned around, and found the black book in his hands. He had torn out a leaf, and before our eyes, black smoke was unfurling across the page, black flowers blossoming, petals wilting, dissolving. I snatched the page from his little hands, and watched rivers and lakes of ink shape into a picture.

What I saw broke my heart.

'I just wanted a piece of paper for a picture,' he lisped at me, thinking his quest for paper had occasioned my anger. I couldn't speak then, tears were choking my throat. I clutched him and buried my face in his nest of curly hair.

'Why are you crying?' he asked. I couldn't tell him.

That night I couldn't sleep, but watched the rise and fall of his chest, as he dreamt. What did he dream? What did six-year-old boys dream of?

It was too much to bear.

My sister came, a couple of days later, to pick up her little son. 'You should spend more time with him,' I told her, gathering his toys together.

My sister wrenched his things out of my hands. 'It's all very well for you to say,' she sneered at me, her voice rising, 'You

don't have a job.' As I started in surprise, she went on, 'Well ...
not a regular job, not like the rest of us. And you don't have a
kid either. Children are expensive—schools, tuitions, nannies,
field trips, summer camp—we have to save for college as well.'
She stormed off, pushing things quickly into his suitcase.

She didn't speak to me for a week.

Perhaps it wouldn't happen, I told myself. Perhaps the
book was wrong.

Some time later, I had a couple of friends over for dinner.
It was a pleasant evening, and as darkness descended, we
uncorked a bottle of wine. It was a night full of stars, and as we
sat outside, a friend began to tell a story about a haunted house
he had lived in. It was a lovely tale, and after that, emboldened
by the magic of the evening and the wine, I started to talk of
the black book.

One of my closest friends, an actor, dismissed my story
with a sweep of his beautiful, elegant hand, and an expression
of derision spreading across his face. 'No! No!' he cried, 'that's
not a story at all. You're a writer—you've got to come up with
something better! With characters, with plot, mystery and
ambition! This is nothing ... too much like Dorian Gray ...' I
was hurt by his flamboyant disapproval, I was a little in love
with him then, many of us were.

Perhaps it was that which made me a little angry.

Incensed, I replied that it wasn't a story, that it was
something true. My audience guffawed, and to prove them
wrong, I rushed into my bedroom and pulled out the book.

My actor friend pried the book loose from my hands. I
watched his perfect, handsome profile, outlined against the

moon, as he flipped through the pages, and watched his smile droop, the light fade from his eyes.

'What is it?' I asked. A strange silence fell over the gathering, as he shut the book, and handed it back to me.

'Nothing, nothing,' he tried to smile, but failed.

I felt a brief flutter of disappointment mingled with guilt—had it been anger, or the wine, that had egged me on? I watched him as he moved away and pulled out a cigarette. As the match flared, the fire lit his face briefly—and I saw something in his expression, that I hadn't seen before—weariness, sadness, disgust? I couldn't tell.

Months later, he lay, sick and wasted, on a hospital bed, diagnosed with AIDS. 'Too much loving,' he told me, a smile twisting his withered lips. I wanted to ask him then, what he had seen in the book, but he turned towards the wall and coughed, blood spewing from his lungs, sores puckering his face. I never got the chance to ask him again.

Ten years passed by.

My sister had moved to the States, years ago, when my nephew had been a scant seven years old. I wanted to tell her then what I had seen, but as the words hovered on my tongue, she spoke first.

'I know what you're going to say,' she told me, 'keep it for yourself. You're not a mother, you don't know what it's like.' She turned, and marched towards her plane.

In America, her family grew, and they prospered—they acquired a house in the country, a number of cars, American citizenship. She made it sound like a perfect life.

But one day, she called me, just as darkness fled from the morning sky. 'He's gone,' she wept, static punctuating her sobs. 'He died, a few hours ago.' Returning from work the previous evening, they had found him, wrists slit, floating in rose-tinted bathwater. It had been too late. The story came out, they—she and her husband—hadn't approved of his clothes, of his friends, of his dreams. 'We didn't understand him,' she cried. I couldn't think of anything to say—I knew they didn't, they hadn't understood him as a six-year-old.

I sat in silence, as day gathered into dusk, and I wondered what I could have said to change things.

And as the call to evening prayer sounded, I pulled on my shoes, and headed for Old Town. I had come here, many times, searching for the same bookshop—but Old Town was a warren of tiny, dark streets, and it was impossible for me to find anything here.

But today I was determined. Perhaps I had to convince myself that I was not guilty. In any case, I chased children as they traipsed across the roofs and alleys of Old Town, watched pigeons swirl high against an orange sky, and listened to the awesome beauty of a imam's prayer, hurtling through a loudspeaker perched on a minaret.

And then I found it, stumbling, almost by mistake, onto the same piles of books lying jumbled on the pavement, just as they had been all those years ago. There was the same darkness inside the shop, the same grimy, yellowing volume of Shakespeare peeking out from under the counter.

Only now, the counter was manned by a young man, smoking a foul smelling cheroot, film music blaring from a mobile phone clipped to his jeans' pocket. Stubble clung to his face, and behind him, on the wall, I could discern a few

pictures, torn from magazines—Salman, Dino, Shah Rukh, the familiar catalogue of film stars.

'Please,' I had asked timidly, 'is the shop owner here?'

He had glared at me, chewing on his cheroot. I pulled out the black book, and showed it to him. 'I bought this ten, eleven years ago, from this shop. I wanted to know ... where it was from.' I gave him a desperate, fervent look, and thought of my nephew, lying palms spread out, in a tub of tepid water.

Something in my expression must have persuaded him, for he turned towards the doorway behind him, and again, like before, shouted 'Ammi!'

And she appeared now, much older.

Her prettiness had faded, her once smooth skin was now mottled and wrinkled. White streaked her hair, but her eyes were just the same—beautiful, grey, almond-shaped eyes—the eyes of a princess, of an houri.

And again, there was the smile—the heart-breaking, beautiful smile.

I placed the book before her. 'I bought this book from this shop many years ago. I was wondering whether anyone could tell me something about it.'

She shook her head. 'If only you had come a few weeks ago,' she said, 'my father died last week. This was his shop, he knew everything about the books here.'

I smiled, regretfully, turning to go, but a thought occurred. 'If you don't mind me asking—how did he die?' I asked.

'Cancer,' she had said. 'Of the lungs. He always said that smoking was going to kill him.' She smiled again, 'It's strange how he knew that.'

That was some time ago. Now, I watch my face age, watch

lines incise themselves onto my skin, watch my cheeks droop, my lips wither. I am growing old, everyone grows old, but I wait for the day when my face will match the face I saw, I still see, in the black book. I keep the book beside me, waiting.

I wait for the fire to come and melt my face, and char the pages of the book.

MIRROR-SELF

Payal Dhar

The only thing Jiya knew about her grandfather was that when he died, her grandmother threw away all the mirrors in her house. She went to see her grandmother at least once a year—mostly during the summer holidays—and must have explored her house top to bottom a thousand times without ever coming across a mirror.

'Appa, why doesn't Paati have mirrors?' she asked her father often.

But Appa only rolled his eyes and said, 'Don't ask.'

So mostly Jiya didn't ask. She loved her Paati very much and basked in the knowledge that she was her favourite granddaughter. She even knew why—it was because she read so much. Paati loved to read too. She had over a thousand books in the 'library' room, and rumour had it that when she was younger, Paati used to write as well.

'What did you write about?' Jiya asked her one time.

'About the truth,' her grandmother replied, after a few moments' thought.

'Oh,' said Jiya, thinking. She had been nine then, about two years ago. 'You mean, you were a journalist?'

Jiya knew all about journalists. Both Amma and Appa worked in the media.

But Paati only laughed and hugged her. 'No, my dear.'

'But why don't you write any more?' persisted Jiya. 'I'd like to read your stories. Were they stories? It doesn't matter, because I like to read all kinds of things. Can I read your stories?'

Then Paati got all serious. 'No, child, you can't. They are too dangerous.'

That sent a thrill up Jiya's spine. How could reading be dangerous? But Paati wouldn't say any more, except mutter something about 'as long as your Thatha was alive.'

While Jiya, her brother, Babu, and their cousins often stayed at Paati's home, she only consented to having them as long as at least one parent stayed. 'I can't manage a group of boisterous children,' she would say irritably.

One of the more malicious aunts whispered something about how the old lady had been slowly losing it after Thatha died, but no one dared openly defy Paati. The only grandchild Paati consented to having with her without any other supervision was Jiya herself. Not even Babu was included. That made Jiya the object of envy among the others, but she didn't care. She loved the house and more than anything else, she loved having Paati all to herself.

But the year that she turned eleven was the last time she stayed there alone.

It was a really old house—older than Paati, and she was so old that she didn't remember her age. Looking up at the ceiling made Jiya dizzy, and she was sometimes scared of the beams running across them. They creaked in complaint with the weight of the fans, and a few times Jiya and Babu had seen squirrels dart in from the garden, sprint across the beams and back, like it was some sort of a dare among themselves. The windows in the house were wide and long, with wooden shutters. Jiya once found it great fun to open and shut the slats of the shutters, but after getting her finger caught she now steered clear of them. The only odd thing about the house was the absence of mirrors. It was exceedingly inconvenient. How was one supposed to brush one's hair, for instance? There was only so much you could do with shiny surfaces and backs of steel plates.

Every afternoon after lunch Paati would shut the windows and pull down the shutters in her bedroom. The room would become dark and then magically cool. Almost as if the scorching summer outside had been banned from entering. Then Paati would perch on her large bed and kick off her slippers. She would take off her glasses, put them on the bedside table, then place her keys next to them. Then she would slowly lie back. Her eyes closed, she would say: 'Jiya, come, lie down for a bit.'

It had always been like that, every day, without fail. And every day, equally without fail, Jiya would wait till her grandmother started snoring softly and then sneak away.

Those two hours that Paati slept was when Jiya lived many adventures—she saved lives, fought aliens, walked on the moon, trawled the oceans for treasure.

The underneath of the gigantic dining table (Paati and Thatha had had seven children!) functioned variously as a secret tunnel, an underground den, the deep seas, a swimming pool, a clearing in a forest, a hut in a rainstorm. A sheet draped over two chairs was her alpine tent where she huddled on cold treacherous nights when the wind screamed outside and wild animals roamed. The heavy bulky furniture formed a dangerous route through enemy territory …

The opportunities were endless. She could be an adventurer, a spy, a detective. She conquered mountains, battled wild beasts and hoodwinked dastardly criminals. A new idea was only a book away, and there were plenty of those about.

But this time it was different. This time Jiya was on a mission: she was going to find out about the mirrors, and she figured that it all had something to do with her grandmother's abandoned writings. A thorough and methodical search of the house—under the pretext of playing adventure games—had led her to the conclusion that whatever secrets lay hidden were inside the room next to her Paati's which was kept locked all the time.

Just before she crept out of the bedroom that fateful afternoon, Jiya made a quick detour to the bedside table and carefully lifted the bunch of keys from the yellowing crocheted cover. She placed a hand under it to keep it from jangling, and watched with bated breath to see if Paati would wake. She didn't, and Jiya escaped.

It was easy to match the number of the golden coloured key that fit the large Godrej padlock. The key turned smooth as butter and before she knew it, Jiya was in what she now thought of as Paati's secret room. And it was such a disappointment.

It was so small that Jiya could almost touch the walls on both sides if she stretched her arms out. About half a dozen steps and she would reach the other end of the narrow room. It was more like a little blind corridor than a room. There were no windows, but strangely there wasn't that musty smell that Jiya remembered when they returned home after a long holiday and the house had been shut up. The room was completely bare except for a rusted metal trunk pushed up against the far wall and a folding ladder—the kind Amma and Appa used to change bulbs or clean the fans. The floor was clean and cool under her bare feet.

Jiya's only hope now was the trunk, but when she went to it, she saw that it had a combination lock. She felt disappointed and annoyed. All that creeping around, and all for nothing. She gave the ladder a little shake in frustration, and as she took another glance around, she looked up at the off-white whitewashed walls reaching up to the ceiling. And something inside her gave a little lurch of excitement.

This ceiling wasn't as high as the others in the house, but there was a loft on the wall to her left. And from where she stood, she could see stacks and stacks of notebooks.

In a frenzy of excitement, Jiya grabbed the ladder and after struggling with it for a while, managed to open it up. She placed it by the wall and climbed up. It wobbled a bit, especially when she reached the top, and for a moment she was sure she would fall. She remained perched on top for a while, crouched, with her hands gripping the little platform on top of the ladder, one foot on the rung just below it. When she felt she had regained her balance, she straightened up slowly.

Oh, but what a disappointment! The loft started at about Jiya's chin level. She could only reach with her arms up to the bottom few books in the piles closest to her. She dared not risk pulling one of them out, for she'd only topple the pile. Bracing her arms on the loft, Jiya started to pull herself up. It was terribly difficult; she was annoyed how the children in the adventure stories she read managed to do this so easily.

Grunting from the effort, Jiya realised she would never pull this off. Her only hope was if she could free one arm and knock one of the books off the pile. She took a deep breath, and gave it all her strength. Heaving herself up, she reached for the closest pile and swiped as hard as she could. There was a flurry of dust and paper, and two of the thin notebooks fluttered down to the floor.

But before she could celebrate, she lost her balance and fell. One of her feet landed hard on the top of the ladder and the other missed it. But she had the presence of mind not to let go of the edge of the loft with her hand, and even as the ladder wobbled dangerously, Jiya hung on.

When her heart stopped feeling like it would burst out of her chest, she gingerly rested her full weight on top of the ladder. The next thing she knew was that she was sailing through the air. There was an almighty crash and for a few seconds Jiya lay on the floor, dazed.

When she realised she was miraculously unhurt, she also figured that Paati would have heard the commotion. She didn't stop to think. She scrambled up, grabbed the two dusty notebooks and fled. She took refuge behind the giant sofa in the living room, and opened the worn, yellowing pages just as she heard voices.

14 December 1976:

This was a completely forgettable experience. And a mistake. I must make a note to never ever target bathroom mirrors again. For one, it was horribly small and cramped, not to mention crowded. For another, and more annoyingly, each time someone came in—apart from myself, that is—I had to turn away.

Ick! Disgusting!

Suffice it to say, I didn't stay in this one very long. And I really don't want to talk about it.

The rest of the notebook was empty. It was an ordinary ruled notebook, similar to the kind Jiya used in school, but with only thirty or so pages in it. It had a thin faded cover with flowers printed on it, and the pages were now disintegrating with age. She turned to the other one. A similar notebook but with the picture of a girl.

8 October 1977:

Sometimes it can be quite a relief to get away. This time I watched the party from the confines of the antique mirror in the hall. And I don't use the term antique lightly. It is so old that the reflection isn't quite what it should be. It was such a relief to literally lie back, knowing that I didn't have to lift a finger to do anything. And yet, no one would miss me. Everyone would see me, greet me, smile at me. Tell me what a wonderful meal it was, and how nice the house looked. And I would smile and thank them …

'Jiya!'

Jiya almost jumped out of her skin. Her grandmother looked down upon her from her not inconsiderable height, hands on her hips.

'Oh … Paati … I …' stammered Jiya, getting to her feet.

'Are you hurt?' Paati interrupted.

'Um … no.'

'You stupid girl!' cried Paati, lightly smacking the side of her head. 'You could have broken something. You could have been seriously hurt! The only reason I have you in the house by yourself is because I know you won't try anything silly. And now look what you've done!'

Jiya stared at the floor miserably.

'And what's that … oh my god! Did you … read?' Paati's voice rose in anger. 'I cannot stand disobedience. Did. You. Read?'

'I'm sorry,' whispered Jiya.

'You should be! I told you it was dangerous and that you were not to read my writing.'

'But it's just words, Paati,' said Jiya before she could stop herself. 'And I didn't really understand.'

Paati let out a long sigh like she was deflating. 'Oh Jiya, you …' She shook her head. 'Come with me.'

She placed a hand on Jiya's shoulder and led her back to the bedroom. They sat side by side on the bed. Jiya hazarded a glance at her grandmother. She didn't seem angry any more, just a little thoughtful and sad.

'I … I am really sorry,' said Jiya again.

Paati sighed again. 'It's all right. You didn't mean any harm.'

'You wrote about mirrors, but you don't like them. How come?'

Paati sat quietly for such a long time that Jiya thought she wouldn't answer.

'Each time we look into a mirror,' said Paati softly, 'we spawn a new self—you could say a copy of ourselves—a mirror-self—carved out of a little bit of our own soul. Every mirror we look into fractures us, little by little by little … That is why some people go senile in their old age. They have looked into too many mirrors in their lifetime, and there's nothing left of them. And each of the mirror-selves, they remain trapped in their own mirrors. They can only go as far as the mirror can see. No further.'

'So you mean every mirror we've ever looked into has a bit of us inside?' asked Jiya incredulously. 'Like a copy of us? A clone?'

'Something like that, yes.'

'But then there must be so, so, so many people inside each mirror. Why can't we see them all?'

'Our mirror-selves only become visible when we ourselves are in its viewing range,' said Paati.

'Oh,' said Jiya, her mind racing. 'What happens to mirrors in shops and things? There must be thousands of people inside them?'

A shiver wracked Paati. 'Yes. There are. Don't ask me. I can't bear to think about it.'

'But Paati, what about those notebooks? You wrote them all, right? There are hundreds of them. Are they all about mirrors?'

Paati sighed. 'Yes, they are. I wrote them when I ... after I ...'

Jiya waited impatiently.

'My children think that I am mad,' said Paati, suddenly changing the subject. To Jiya's alarm, a tear rolled down her cheek. 'They don't believe me.'

Jiya took the old woman's hand. It was wrinkly and spotted, but soft and warm. 'But I believe you, Paati.'

Paati squeezed her hand and smiled through her tears. 'Yes, I know that, and that's why I'm going to tell you, but will you promise me not to tell anyone?'

'I promise,' said Jiya solemnly.

'I know how to get inside mirrors,' was Paati's next surprising confession. Jiya's eyes went round, but her grandmother didn't stop. 'And when you enter a mirror, you free your mirror-self from there and take its place. Each of those notebooks you saw contains an account of each time I entered a mirror.'

Jiya gasped. 'You mean you did it many times?'

Paati nodded. 'Four hundred and seventy-eight times. I let four hundred and seventy-seven mirror-selves of mine experience freedom for a short time.'

'How did you come out? If it's that easy to come out, wouldn't all our mirror-selves ... er ... escape?'

'Oh no,' said Paati. 'They don't have an anchor to the real world, you see. Me—I had your Thatha. He was the only one who didn't think I was insane. Each time I went into a mirror he said he would be waiting for me to come back, and each time I did ... I could.'

'But when Thatha died …'

'I had nothing left to come back to,' finished Paati.

Jiya's heart was racing. 'You said four hundred and seventy-eight times, but four hundred and seventyseven mirror-selves. Does that mean …'

Paati was nodding slowly. 'I am the four hundred and seventy-eighth.' She smiled, but this time Jiya didn't find the smile warm and loving.

'And I remain free.'

NO LIVING VOICE

Thomas Street Millington

ow do you account for it?'

'I don't account for it at all. I don't pretend to understand it.'

'You think, then, that it was really supernatural?'

'We know so little what Nature comprehends what are its powers and limits that we can scarcely speak of anything that happens as beyond it or above it.'

'And you are certain that this did happen?'

'Quite certain; of that I have no doubt whatsoever.'

These sentences passed between two gentlemen in the drawing room of a country house, where a small family party was assembled after dinner; and in consequence of a lull in the conversation occurring at the moment they were distinctly heard by nearly everybody present. Curiosity was excited, and enquiries were eagerly pressed as to the nature or supernature of the event under discussion. 'A ghost story!' cried one; 'Oh!

Delightful! We must and will hear it.' 'Oh! Please, no, said another, 'I should not sleep all night and yet I am dying with curiosity.'

Others seemed inclined to treat the question rather from a rational or psychological point of view, and would have started a discussion upon ghosts in general, each giving his own experience; but these were brought back by the voice of the hostess, crying, 'Question, question!' and the first speakers were warmly urged to explain what particular event had formed the subject of their conversation.

'It was you, Mr Browne, who said you could not account for it; and you are such a very matter-of-fact person that we feel doubly anxious to hear what wonderful occurrence could have made you look so grave and earnest.'

'Thank you,' said Mr Browne. 'I *am* a matter-of-fact person, I confess; and I was speaking of a fact; though I must beg to be excused saying any more about it. It is an old story; but I never even think of it without a feeling of distress; and I should not like to stir up such keen and haunting memories merely for the sake of gratifying curiosity. I was relating to Mr Smith, in few words, an adventure which befell me in Italy many years ago, giving him the naked facts of the case, in refutation of a theory which he had been propounding.'

'Now we don't want theories, and we won't have naked facts; they are hardly proper at any time, and at this period of the year, with snow upon the ground, they would be most unseasonable; but we must have that story fully and feelingly related to us, and we promise to give it a respectful hearing, implicit belief, and unbounded sympathy. So draw round the fire, all of you, and let Mr Browne begin.'

Poor Mr Browne turned pale and red, his lips quivered, his entreaties to be excused became quite plaintive; but his good nature and perhaps, also, the consciousness that he could really interest his hearers, led him to overcome his reluctance; and after exacting a solemn promise that there should be no jesting or levity in regard to what he had to tell, he cleared his throat twice or thrice, and in a hesitating nervous tone began as follows:

'It was in the spring of 18. I had been at Rome during the Holy Week, and had taken a place in the diligence for Naples. There were two routes: one by way of Terracina and the other by the Via Latina, more inland. The diligence, which made the journey only twice a week, followed these routes alternately, so that each road was traversed only once in seven days. I chose the inland route, and after a long day's journey arrived at Ceprano, where we halted for the night.

The next morning we started again very early, and it was scarcely yet daylight when we reached the Neapolitan frontier, at a short distance from the town. There our passports were examined, and to my great dismay I was informed that mine was not *en regle*. It was covered, indeed, with stamps and signatures, not one of which had been procured without some cost and trouble; but one visa yet was wanting, and that the all-important one, without which none could enter the kingdom of Naples. I was obliged therefore to alight, and to send my wretched passport back to Rome, my wretched self being doomed to remain under police surveillance at Ceprano, until the diligence should bring it back to me on that day week, at soonest.

I took up my abode at the hotel where I had passed the previous night, and there I presently received a visit from the *Capo di Polizia*, who told me very civilly that I must present myself, every morning and evening at his bureau, but that I might have liberty to 'circulate' in the neighbourhood during the day. I grew so weary of this dull place, that after I had explored the immediate vicinity of the town I began to extend my walks to a greater distance, and as I always reported myself to the police before night I met with no objection on their part.

One day, however, when I had been as far as Alatri and was returning on foot, night overtook me. I had lost my way, and could not tell how far I might be from my destination. I was very tired and had a heavy knapsack on my shoulders, packed with stones and relics from the ruins of the old Pelasgic fortress which I had been exploring, besides a number of old coins and a lamp or two which I had purchased there. I could discern no signs of any human habitation, and the hills, covered with wood, seemed to shut me in on every side. I was beginning to think seriously of looking out for some sheltered spot under a thicket in which to pass the night, when the welcome sound of a footstep behind me fell upon my ears. Presently a man dressed in the usual long shaggy coat of a shepherd overtook me, and hearing of my difficulty offered to conduct me to a house at a short distance from the road, where I might obtain a lodging; before we reached the spot he told me that the house in question was an inn and that he was the landlord of it. He had not much custom, he said, so he employed himself in shepherding during the day; but he could make me comfortable, and give me a good supper also, better than I should expect, to look at him; but he had been in different circumstances once, and had lived in service in good families, and knew how things ought to be, and what a *signor* like myself was used to.

'The house to which he took me seemed like its owner to have seen better days. It was a large rambling place and much dilapidated, but it was tolerably comfortable within; and my landlord, after he had thrown off his sheepskin coat, prepared me a good and savoury meal, and sat down to look at and converse with me while I ate it. I did not much like the look of the fellow; but he seemed anxious to be sociable and told me a great deal about his former life when he was in service, expecting to receive similar confidences from me. I did not gratify him much, but one must talk of something, and he seemed to think it only proper to express an interest in his guests and to learn as much of their concerns as they would tell him.

'I went to bed early, intending to resume my journey as soon as it should be light. My landlord took up my knapsack, and carried it to my room, observing as he did so that it was a great weight for me to travel with. I answered jokingly that it contained great treasures, referring to my coins and relics; of course he did not understand me, and before I could explain he wished me a most happy little night, and left me.

'The room in which I found myself was situated at the end of a long passage; there were two rooms on the right side of this passage, and a window on the left, which looked out upon a yard or garden. Having taken a survey of the outside of the house while smoking my cigar after dinner, when the moon was up, I understood exactly the position of my chamber—the end room of a long narrow wing, projecting at right angles from the main building, with which it was connected only by the passage and the two side rooms already mentioned.

Please bear this description carefully in mind while I proceed.

'Before getting into bed, I drove into the floor close to the door a small gimlet which formed part of a complicated pocket-knife which I always carried with me, so that it would be impossible for any one to enter the room without my knowledge; there was a lock to the door, but the key would not turn in it; there was also a bolt, but it would not enter the hole intended for it, the door having sunk apparently from its proper level. I satisfied, myself, however, that the door was securely fastened by my gimlet, and soon fell asleep.

'How can I describe the strange and horrible sensation which oppressed me as I woke out of my first slumber? I had been sleeping soundly, and before I quite recovered consciousness I had instinctively risen from my pillow, and was crouching forward, my knees drawn up, my hands clasped before my face, and my whole frame quivering with horror. I saw nothing, felt nothing; but a sound was ringing in my ears which seemed to make my blood run cold. I could not have supposed it possible that any mere sound, whatever might be its nature, could have produced such a revulsion of feeling or inspired such intense horror as I then experienced. It was not a cry of terror that I heard that would have roused me to action nor the moaning of one in pain that would have distressed me, and called forth sympathy rather than aversion. True, it was like the groaning of one in anguish and despair, but not like any mortal voice: it seemed too dreadful, too intense, for human utterance. The sound had begun while I was fast asleep close in the head of my bed, close to my very pillow; it continued after I was wide awake—a long, loud, hollow, protracted groan, making the midnight air reverberate, and then dying gradually away until it ceased entirely. It was some minutes before I could at all recover from the terrible impression which seemed to stop my breath and paralyse my limbs. At length I began to look about me, for the night was not entirely dark, and I could discern the outlines of the room and the several pieces of furniture in it. I then got out of bed, and called aloud, "Who is there? What is the matter? Is anyone ill?" I repeated these enquiries in Italian and in French, but there was none that answered.

Fortunately I had some matches in my pocket and was able to light my candle. I then examined every pan of the room carefully, and especially the wall at the head of my bed, sounding it with my knuckles; it was firm and solid there, as in all other places. I unfastened my door, and explored the passage and the two adjoining rooms, which were unoccupied and almost destitute of furniture; they had evidently not been used for some time. Search as I would I could gain no clue to the mystery. Returning to my room I sat down upon the bed in great perplexity, and began to turn over in my mind whether it was possible I could have been deceived whether the sounds which caused me such distress might be the offspring of some dream or nightmare; but to that conclusion I could not bring myself at all, much as I wished it, for the groaning had continued ringing in my ears long after I was wide awake and conscious. While I was thus reflecting, having neglected to close the door which was opposite to the side of my bed where I was sitting, I heard a soft footstep at a distance, and presently a light appeared at the further end of the passage.

Then I saw the shadow of a man east upon the opposite wall; it moved very slowly, and presently stopped. I saw the hand raised, as if making a sign to someone, and I knew from the fact of the shadow being thrown in advance that there must be a second person in the rear by whom the light was earned. After a short pause they seemed to retrace their steps, without my having had a glimpse of either of them, but only of the shadow which had come before and which followed them as they withdrew. It was then a little after one o'clock, and I concluded they were retiring late to rest, and anxious to avoid disturbing me, though I have since thought that it was the light from my room which caused their retreat. I felt half inclined to call to them, but I shrank, without knowing why, from making known what had disturbed me, and while I hesitated they were gone; so I fastened my door again, and resolved to sit up and watch a little longer by myself.

But now my candle was beginning to burn low, and I found myself in this dilemma: either I must extinguish it at once, or I should be left without the means of procuring a light in ease I should be again disturbed. I regretted that I had not called for another candle while there were people yet moving in the house, but I could not do so now without making explanations; so I grasped my box of matches, put out my light, and lay down, not without a shudder, in the bed.

'For an hour or more I lay awake thinking over what had occurred, and by that time I had almost persuaded myself that I had nothing but my own morbid imagination to thank for the alarm which I had suffered. "It is an outer wall," I said to myself; "they are all outer walls, and the house is built of stone; it is impossible that any sound could be heard through such a thickness. Besides, it seemed to be in my room, close to my ear.

What an idiot I must be, to be excited and alarmed about nothing; I'll think no more about it." So I turned on my side, with a smile (rather a forced one) at my own foolishness, and composed myself to sleep.

'At that instant I heard, with more distinctness than I ever heard any other sound in my life, a gasp, a voiceless gasp, as if someone were in agony for breath, biting at the air, or trying with desperate efforts to cry out or speak. It was repeated a second and a third time; then there was a pause; then again that horrible gasping; and then a long-drawn breath, an audible drawing up of the air into the throat, such as one would make in heaving a deep sigh. Such sounds as these could not possibly have been heard unless they had been close to my ear; they seemed to come from the wall at my head, or to rise up out of my pillow.

That fearful gasping, and that drawing in of the breath, in the darkness and silence of the night, seemed to make every nerve in my body thrill with dreadful expectation. Unconsciously I shrank away from it, crouching down as before, with my face upon my knees. It ceased, and immediately a moaning sound began, which lengthened out into an awful, protracted groan, waxing louder and louder, as if under an increasing agony, and then dying away slowly and gradually into silence; yet painfully and distinctly audible even to the last.

'As soon as I could rouse myself from the freezing horror which seemed to penetrate even to my joints and marrow, I crept away from the bed, and in the furthest corner of the room lit my candle, looking anxiously about me as I did so, expecting some dreadful revelation as the light flashed up.

Yet, if you will believe me, I did not feel alarmed or frightened; but rather oppressed, and penetrated with an unnatural, overpowering, sentiment of awe. I seemed to be in the presence of some great and horrible mystery, some bottomless depth of woe, or misery, or crime. I shrank from it with a sensation of intolerable loathing and suspense. It was a feeling akin to this which prevented me from calling to my landlord. I could not bring myself to speak to him of what had passed; not knowing how nearly he might be himself involved in the mystery. I was only anxious to escape as quietly as possible from the room and from the house. The candle was now beginning to flicker in its socket, but the stars were shining outside, and there was space and air to breathe there, which seemed to be wanting in my room; so I hastily opened my window, tied the bedclothes together for a rope, and lowered myself silently and safely to the ground.

'There was a light still burning in the lower part of the house; but I crept noiselessly along, feeling my way carefully among the trees, and in due time came upon a beaten track which led me to a road, the same which I had been travelling on the previous night. I walked on, scarcely knowing whither, anxious only to increase my distance from the accursed house, until the day began to break, when almost the first object I could see distinctly was a small body of men approaching me. It was with no small pleasure that I recognised at their head my friend the *Capo di Polizia*. "Ah!" he cried, "unfortunate *Inglese*, what trouble you have given me!

Where have you been? God be praised that I see you safe and sound! But how? What is the matter with you?

You look like one possessed."

'I told him how I had lost my way, and where I had lodged.

"And what happened to you there?" he cried, with a look of anxiety.

"I was disturbed in the night. I could not sleep. I made my escape, and here I am. I cannot tell you more."

"But you must tell me more, dear sir; forgive me; you must tell me everything. I must know all that passed in that house. We have had it under our surveillance for a long time, and when I heard in what direction you had gone yesterday, and had not returned, I feared you had got into some mischief there, and we were even now upon our way to look for you."

'I could not enter into particulars, but I told him I had heard strange sounds, and at his request I went back with him to the spot. He told me by the way that the house was known to be the resort of *banditti*; that the landlord harboured them, received their ill-gotten goods, and helped them to dispose of their booty.

'On arriving at the spot, he placed his men about the premises and instituted a strict search, the landlord and the man who was found in the house being compelled to accompany him. The room in which I had slept was carefully examined; the floor was of plaster or cement, so that no sound could have passed through it; the walls were sound and solid, and there was nothing to be seen that could in any way account for the strange disturbance I had experienced. The room on the ground-floor underneath my bedroom was next inspected; it contained a quantity of straw, hay, firewood, and lumber. It was paved with brick, and on turning over the straw which was heaped together in a corner it was observed that the bricks were uneven, as if they had been recently disturbed.

"Dig here," said the officer, "we shall find something hidden here, I imagine."

'The landlord was evidently much disturbed. "Stop," he cried. "I will tell you what lies there; come away out of doors, and you shall know all about it."

"Dig, I say. We will find out for ourselves."

"Let the dead rest," cried the landlord, with a trembling voice. "For the love of heaven come away, and hear what I shall tell you."

"Go on with your work," said the sergeant to his men, who were now plying pickaxe and spade.

"I can't stay here and see it," exclaimed the landlord once more. "Hear then! It is the body of my son, my only son let him rest, if rest he can. He was wounded in a quarrel, and brought home here to die. I thought he would recover, but there was neither doctor nor priest at hand, and in spite of all that we could do for him he died. Let him alone now, or let a priest first be sent for; he died unconfessed, but it was not my fault; it may not be yet too late to make peace for him."

"But why is he buried in this place?"

"We did not wish to make a stir about it. Nobody knew of his death, and we laid him down quietly; one place I thought was as good as another when once the life was out of him. We are poor folk, and could not pay for ceremonies." The truth at length came out. Father and son were both members of a band of thieves; under this floor they concealed their plunder, and there too lay more than one mouldering corpse, victims who had occupied the room in which I slept, and had there met their death. The son was indeed buried in that spot; he had been mortally wounded in a skirmish with travellers, and had lived long enough to repent of his deeds and to beg for that priestly absolution which, according to his creed, was necessary to secure his pardon.

In vain he had urged his father to bring the confessor to his bedside; in vain he had entreated him to break off from the murderous band with which he was allied and to live honestly in future; his prayers were disregarded, and his dying admonitions were of no avail. But for the strange mysterious warning which had roused me from my sleep and driven me out of the house that night another crime would have been added to the old man's tale of guilt. That gasping attempt to speak, and that awful groaning, whence did they proceed?

It was no living voice. Beyond that I will express no opinion on the subject. I will only say it was the means of saving my life, and at the same time putting an end to the series of bloody deeds which had been committed in that house.

'I received my passport that evening by the diligence from Rome, and started the next morning on my way to Naples. As we were crossing the frontier a tall figure approached, wearing the long rough *cappoua* of the mendicant friars, with a hood over the face and holes for the eyes to look through. He carried a tin money-box in his hand, which he held out to the passengers, jingling a few coins in it, and crying in a monotonous voice, "*Anime in purgatorio! Anime in purgatorio!*"

I do not believe in purgatory, nor in supplications for the dead; but I dropped a piece of silver into the box nevertheless, as I thought of that unhallowed grave in the forest, and my prayer went up to heaven in all sincerity "*Requiescat in pace!*"'

THE VOICE

Tanvi Mehta

I wake up with a headache that won't go away. Trying to ignore it, I go about getting ready as usual—but my body just feels unfamiliar. Standing in front of the mirror to brush my teeth, I raise my toothbrush up to my mouth—and miss it completely. *I don't remember my mouth being that high.* Or at least my hand doesn't. Maybe I slept in a bad position and my arm is just stiff. Shrugging, I get dressed—*my pants seem a bit too long, my shirt too roomy*—and head out the door, reaching for a granola bar on the way. Something feels odd.

I haven't slept very well; everything seems like a dream to me. Eyes, far too big for faces, beam at me disconcertingly. Movements seem unnaturally glitchy almost. Voices are just a little bit off pitch. I walk—*stumble?*—through my day, because coffee does nothing for me. The world just has an uncomfortable film over it.

Everything is far too quiet when I get home. I notice it immediately. I can suddenly hear my footsteps echoing through the house, getting louder and louder inside my mind, an uneasy, fearful feeling rising in my gut—*inexplicable.* I can feel the silence on my face, pressing gently, my skin tingling. Why does everything feel so odd?

Someone is following me. No. Nobody behind, nobody in any of the rooms. No shadows in the mirrors, no people in the dark corners. I check everything. What is it then, what's making the hair on the back of my neck stand? What is that eerie tickle I feel on my back, like someone is watching me? I can't shake off the feeling that *something is wrong.*

I sit down and turn on the TV, trying to dose off, drown out the white noise in my ears, but somehow I'm hyper aware of everything suddenly. My eyes dart around the room—and then I realise what it is. *The room seems smaller. My furniture is closer together.* I could've sworn there was at least two feet between the couch and the coffee table, but now they're almost touching. I blink—*and it's back to normal.*

Unsettled and undeniably uncomfortable, I decide to sleep off this strange state of mind. I get into bed—*and I can swear the room moves around me.* In immediate response, my bookshelf creaks just slightly, as if the weight it put on the wall is now on its legs. I have to believe this is in my head. I flip the light switch, and my hand drops down. There is a foot between the shelf and the wall. I don't know what to do. I sit and stare at the new space in petrified silence—what is happening to me?

I'm sure I'm imagining it. Furniture doesn't move. Walls don't either. But *why is there a space? Why can I see it?* I walk over and slip behind the bookshelf. An unearthly cold fills the space, and I can feel the goosebumps rise all over me. I don't know what else to do, so I go back to bed. Somehow I feel more comfortable with the lights off. I lie there, silent and unmoving, unsure of what to do, staring at the ceiling. And then I hear it. At first, it's soft, almost non-existent, but then it gets louder, echoing through the house—a woman's cry, broken and miserable, getting shriller and shriller until she is wailing—a blood-curdling, endless shriek. I follow the noise to its origin—*the wall*. Terror grips my throat. Something is in my house. Something is moving my walls, and there is nothing I can do about it. All I can do is watch the darkness, watch my walls, knowing that they're moving. I'm powerless. I could leave—but can I? I can't possibly walk through this abyss. I stare for hours at the dark space behind my bookshelf, until I slump back against the wall, asleep.

In the morning, I force myself to leave, to continue normally. My mind whirs endlessly; days pass uneventfully after this, but I can't focus on them anymore. I can't do anything. I go through the motions of my routine mindlessly, constantly glancing at the walls, making sure they're in the same place as they were a minute ago. Nothing new happens, but I'm paranoid—the thought has infested my mind, burrowing, making a home inside the pit of my brain, nestling comfortably, refusing to move. And then it happens again, just as I'm beginning to forget.

I'm in bed, staring at the walls blankly, when my bed groans, just slightly, but enough to be heard in the silence. I'm awake immediately. Lights on, I look around, almost reluctant to see what the movement was. I know before I see it. *There is a space right behind my bed.* The back wall has moved. I'm stiff, stuck to the bed, unable to do anything but turn off the lights and lie down, nerves on end, almost anticipating something, anything—but nothing happens.

I'm useless against whatever this is—all I can do is wait for this *thing* to close in on me, soundless, just out of sight, but moving.

I know it's there, I can almost feel it stroking my neck, right at the jugular with its nails—or are they teeth—teasing me. I can hear its silent laugh, and I know I should be running, or flinching at least, but I can't do anything, not even shiver at its touch, this unknown, unearthly creature. I spend the whole night waiting—but nothing happens. I sit, watching my walls, now home to this *creature,* the breath and blood pulsating in the life behind them, in this *thing* that sits somewhere in the dark, watching me like I watch the walls—only *amused* at me.

Morning comes—and with light comes sleep. In the light, I know somehow that it can't do anything—walls don't move in the day. I wake up hours later with a start—plates are crashing in the kitchen and I have a sinking feeling about it. Sure enough, something is wrong. Very wrong. The entire cupboard of plates is missing, with only a blank wall in its place. The plates continue to crash *behind the wall* for a minute—and then silence.

I've had enough. I force myself to leave the house. Outside feels safe, good almost. I take a long, forcedly relaxed walk around the mall, stopping at the electronics store to pick up the highest quality video cameras I can afford. Then I get food—I've barely eaten in days, I realise, and sit at my table, deciding to stay until I'm asked to leave, because I know if

I go outside *It* will tempt me back, pull at my curiosity, slip its nails under my skin and tug just slightly, and I will have to go back.

Eventually, I head home. I set up the cameras in each room—if something is moving my walls I'd like to see it. Then, I measure. I spend hours drawing out a detailed plan of the house, marking every dimension carefully, measuring each length again and again until I've convinced myself—until I've convinced *It*—that I'm sure. The plates are back, unbroken, inside their cupboard, which has reappeared somehow. *What is happening to me?*

After I'm done, I sit aimlessly, unable to do anything but watch the walls, wait for something to happen, for *It* to show itself, because I know it's there, behind my walls, watching me, laughing at my futile efforts to track *It*, to see what its plan is for me, for this house. *It* knows I'm useless, that nothing I do will help me, that I'm so stupid, *so stupid for even trying.* Not even the TV will drown out the white noise anymore, so I just wait for *It* to show itself somewhere, in some wall or shelf— because what else can I do? I'm resigned to simply sitting here, attending to *Its* twisted smile, its unearthly scream, so high-pitched and unnatural that it's only in my head that I can hear it. I can't leave this house, not for anything, because what would *It* do without me? *It* thrives off me, it lives off my very existence, and without me, who will show the world what *It* is?

Hours pass. Nothing has moved. I'm beginning to get impatient, so I check. I measure every length, every corner. I walk past every shelf, looking, desperately for change. I pace around and around the house, one shoulder dragging against the wall—leaning, but still moving, staring at the floor—what if that moves and suddenly there's just empty space below me? I listen to the walls, one ear pressed against the painted smoothness, under which I know lives a living, breathing being, and I can hear the voices, the whispers and moans, the *cries* of the people it's seen and laughed at—because I can't be the only one—the ones it's crept up behind and slowly but deliberately sucked the life out of through the mind—and I'm lying on the floor now, dragging myself, because I need to be touching as much of the house as I can, I need to *feel* Its presence, and lying down allows me that—greater surface area, you see, and I strain my ears to hear that soft cry that tells me that *It* is back—knowing where It is makes me feel better I think.

And then the screaming is back, and it's filling my head, filling my nerves, and numbing my senses so I won't feel It coming when it does. I keep crawling, keep trying to follow the sound that's moving around so fast all of a sudden—and then I'm scratching at the walls, trying to find It, needing to see It. I take a knife from the kitchen and start hacking at my walls, and suddenly they're all moving, the whole house is changing shape and all that stays constant is the wall I'm attacking—and I see it, empty eyes staring at me, a demonic smile twisting whatever face it has, bony hands reaching for me, leaving dark red scratches across my skin as the panic sets in and I try to fight back. I can't breathe, its face leaning in, closer and closer, until I can feel its breath on my neck, its nails drawing blood across my face. Wordlessly, It pulls me into its hole, into the cold, swampy darkness behind the walls, and all I can hear is the screaming inside my head, inside *Its* head, as everything goes black.

I wake up in agony, on the floor next to the wall. Stiff and in pain, I get up and look at myself in the mirror—and my stomach drops. Cuts adorn my face—but they are clean and precise. *I have been cut only by a knife.*

The wall is untouched. *The bookshelf has been pushed forward.* Only the bloody knife with my blood all over it lies on the floor where I woke up.

THE HUNGARIAN DOLL

Shreya Kaushik

uess who's back!' Alia called out with a laugh as she walked through the door of her sister's home.

Anita turned from the kitchen counter, a smile swiftly making its way across her face as she reached out to embrace her sister.

'Well, it's been long enough!' she chuckled. 'How was Hungary?'

'Beautiful, like the travel advisor said. The castles were absolutely stunning, Didi. I wish you could have seen them.'

Anita smiled softly. 'You're the gypsy in the family, not me. How long are you back in Mumbai for?'

'A week, just to tie up some work and submit the article. Then I'm off to Alexandria,' Alia grinned, making herself comfortable on an old armchair. Anita was right—she *was* like a gypsy. She had studied Economics in college, before

she'd realised that her thirst for adventure meant that she just wasn't cut out for a desk job.

After that, it had only been a few months before she'd turned her interest to photography, and started to yearn for the sights and sounds of other cities. Mumbai was home, but she had a keen desire to explore the world. After graduating, she'd gotten a job working as a photographer for a prominent magazine. Now, she could travel *and* make a living from it.

She loved her sister and her niece, and Mumbai *was* home, but travelling was in her blood as much as domesticity was in her sister's.

'Hi Maasi!' an excited little voice piped up, bringing her out of her reverie. She looked down with a wide grin at the six-year-old girl with wild curls.

'Hello, Ayesha. Did you come to see me only because I have presents?'

'Presents!' the little girl gasped, excitement lighting up her small face. 'Where, Maasi? Show me!'

Alia reached down into her bag, pulling out a square-shaped box. 'There you ...' she laughed, barely able to finish before Ayesha let out an excited squeal and grabbed the box from her hand.

Anita chuckled. 'You shouldn't spoil her so much. She doesn't need so many presents, you know.'

'Nonsense! Every child does. Who else could I buy toys for?'

'Oooohhhh!' Ayesha exclaimed. 'I've never seen a doll with a frowning face before!'

'That's why I thought you'd like it, baby. Do you?'

Ayesha nodded fervently, lifting the doll up so her mother

could see it. Anita's face became troubled as she looked at it.  'Alia, this looks too expensive—you shouldn't have.'

'It wasn't *that* expensive, Didi. I know how to bargain, remember? Besides, she likes it.'

'She's only six,' Anita said quietly. 'She might ruin it.'

'Then it's hers to ruin,' Alia said, trying to forget how Anita's words made her remember her experience when she had bought the doll.

'I'll take that one,' she had said, pointing to a doll with a particularly lavish dress, drawn to the odd frown on its face.

The shopkeeper smiled at her, handing over the doll in a bag. 'You are a collector, yes?' she asked, her accent heavy.

Alia smiled back. 'No, the doll is for my niece.'

The old woman's posture changed; Alia could have sworn that her back stiffened. 'How ... how old is your niece?' she asked, her tone deceptively casual.

'Six.'

Now her posture definitely changed; her face turned pale, her lips white with fear, as she muttered in Hungarian.

'Sorry?' Alia asked, confused.

'You must not give the doll to a child,' the woman said desperately.

'Please, you must not give the doll to a child!'

Alia stared at her in confusion and a little alarm, quickly turning to leave. The woman was probably crazy, she told herself. She wasn't exactly young.

With a quick shake of her head, she turned back to Anita. 'Let her keep it,' she repeated. 'Whom will it hurt?'

***

The next day, Alia walked back into Anita's house. 'I had some time to kill before going into the office.' She looked around. 'Where's Ayesha?'

'Still asleep,' Anita said tersely. 'She didn't get much sleep last night. She came into my room at about two.'

'Oh, what happened?'

'She had a nightmare,' Anita said with a shake of her head. 'She said the doll was going to eat her.'

Alia's head whipped up from the newspaper she had been reading. *'What?'* she choked out, her mind filled with the image of the shopkeeper's fear-stricken face.

Anita looked at her in amusement. 'Don't worry, this happens all the time. Just last week she had a dream that her teddy bear wanted her to drink tea,' she rolled her eyes. 'She doesn't like tea.'

Ayesha walked into the room then, rubbing her eyes sleepily with one little knuckle, the doll tucked under her other arm.

'What's all this about a nightmare, sweetheart?' Alia asked, her voice falsely cheery.

Ayesha shook her head. 'Wasn't a nightmare, Maasi,' she said.

'Elizabeth *did* say she was going to eat me.'

'Elizabeth?' Alia whispered to Anita.

'She says the doll told her that her name was Elizabeth,' Anita whispered back.

Alia cleared her throat. 'Shall I take Elizabeth back? If she's saying those things?'

Ayesha shook her head, her eyes oddly dreamy. 'Elizabeth doesn't want to leave,' she said. 'She wants to stay.'

Alia cast an unsure look at the doll. 'Well, all right then,' she said. 'I should go to work now. I'll see you both in the evening!'

As she walked out, trying to clear her head, no one but the little girl noticed the shadow that ever so briefly flickered across the apartment walls.

***

At six in the evening, when Alia walked in, Ayesha was playing with the doll on the floor. 'She had the dream again, this afternoon,'

Anita whispered. 'I'm not sure why—maybe it's one of those recurring childhood dreams.'

'Probably,' Alia agreed, trying to shake off the distinct feeling of unease. 'Maybe it's because the doll frowns.'

'Its dress is lovely though, isn't it? Such intricate embroidery, especially that crest at the back.'

'Crest?' Alia said in surprise, looking over at the doll in Ayesha's hands.

Her eyes lighted on an intricately woven pattern on its back, which quite clearly was a family crest of some sort. Underneath the crest, in neat little stitches, were the initials 'E B'.

***

Alia lay awake that night, unable to stop thinking about the doll. Yes, it had seemed normal enough when she had bought it, but now … something wasn't right about it. And she didn't think the nightmares Ayesha was having were normal, either.

With a sigh, she got out of bed and pulled her laptop towards her, deciding that trying to get answers would help her more than sleeping.

Hardly detective work, she thought wryly to herself, as she googled 'old Hungarian family crests' images, and was rewarded with a slew of pictures. A few rows down, she found one identical to the crest on the doll's back.

'Nadasdy family crest', said the inscription at the bottom.

Remembering the initials on the doll, she typed 'E B Nadasdy' into the search engine.

The result she clicked on nearly made her gasp in terror.

'Elizabeth Bathory, Countess Nadasdy', read the Wikipedia page, the picture that of an attractive woman in her mid-twenties, but with cold, darkly cruel eyes. *'History's Most Prolific Serial Killer'*.

Cold, icy fingers of fear gripped Alia's heart as she read on.

Elizabeth Bathory was a prominent Hungarian noblewoman in the sixteenth century, and had been obsessed with staying young. One day, after slapping a maidservant in a fit of anger, the girl's blood had splashed her arm; that patch of skin looked more radiant than the rest of her arm after she'd washed it. Convinced that blood was the elixir of eternal youth, Elizabeth had begun to murder young adolescent girls, scarcely older than ten or eleven, and bathe in their blood. Occasionally, she would even drink it.

It didn't take long before the authorities caught on to what was happening; Elizabeth was arrested, and imprisoned in a small brick room in her own castle. With nothing else to do, she passed her time reading and sewing. Mostly she sewed dolls, but she sewed frowns on instead of smiles as a symbol of the humiliation she had suffered.

Before her death, she had sworn revenge on all who had captured her, declaring that the killings would never stop.

Legend has it that her spirit transferred itself into the dolls she had sewn, trapped in their eternal state of misery.

Alia leapt up, unable to stifle a terrified scream at the gruesome tale. *That* was why the shopkeeper had begged her not to give the doll to a child; Elizabeth's victims had been young girls!

Blind to everything else, Alia sped out of the house towards her car. She *had* to get to Ayesha and Anita in time, and destroy the doll before anything could happen.

She drove like a madwoman, thanking her stars fervently that the policemen were still asleep, and there was no one to stop her or slow her down.

By the time she reached Anita's house, the sun was just beginning to rise. Ignoring the tranquillity of the scene in favour of the terror raging in her heart, she raced up the stairs to their front door.

'Didi!' she screamed, pounding on the door as hard as she could. When no one answered, she summoned all her strength and flung herself against the door, feeling it give way just as she felt her shoulder disconnect from its socket from the impact. Ignoring the searing pain, she ran as fast as she could to Ayesha's bedroom.

As she ran in, her blood turned to ice; Anita stood weeping on the side of the bed, shaking a still Ayesha.

On the side of the little girl's neck was a long slit; her body was white, clearly drained of all its blood.

'Ayesha, wake up!' Anita sobbed. 'Please, wake up!'

Alia sank to her knees, hot tears falling on to her cheeks, hardly able to believe that she was too late.

Suddenly, just beyond Anita, she caught sight of the doll on the shelf.

Before her horrified gaze, it turned its face towards her with a terrifying slowness, a perfect, crimson drop of blood beginning to drip from its now-smiling mouth.

THE SHADOW

Edith Nesbitt

This is not an artistically rounded off ghost story, and nothing is explained in it, and there seems to be no reason why any of it should have happened. But that is no reason why it should not be told. You must have noticed that all the real ghost stories you have ever come close to, are like this in these respects—no explanation, no logical coherence. Here is the story.

There were three of us and another, but she had fainted suddenly at the second extra of the Christmas dance, and had been put to bed in the dressing room next to the room which we three shared. It had been one of those jolly, old fashioned dances where nearly everybody stays the night, and the big country house is stretched to its utmost containing—guests harbouring on sofas, couches, settees, and even mattresses on floors. Some of the young men actually, I believe, slept on the great dining table.

We had talked of our partners, as girls will, and then the stillness of the manor house, broken only by the whisper of the wind in the cedar branches, and the scraping of their harsh fingers against our window panes, had pricked us to such luxurious confidence in our surroundings of bright chintz and candle-flame and fire-light, that we had dared to talk of ghosts—in which, we all said, we did not believe one bit. We had told the story of the phantom coach, and the horribly strange bed, and the lady in the sacque, and the house in Berkeley Square.

None of us believed in ghosts, but my heart, at least, seemed to leap to my throat and choke me there, when a tap came to our door—a faint tap, not to be mistaken.

'Who's there?' said the youngest of us, craning a lean neck towards the door. It opened slowly, and I give you my word the instant of suspense that followed is still reckoned among my life's least confident moments. Almost at once the door opened fully, and Miss Eastwich, my aunt's housekeeper, companion and general stand-by, looked in on us.

We all said 'Come in,' but she stood there. She was, at all normal hours, the most silent woman I have ever known. She stood and looked at us, and shivered a little. So did we—for in those days corridors were not warmed by hot-water pipes, and the air from the door was keen.

'I saw your light,' she said at last, 'and I thought it was late for you to be up—after all this gaiety. I thought perhaps —' her glance turned towards the door of the dressing room. 'No,' I said, 'she's fast asleep.' I should have added a goodnight, but the youngest of us forestalled my speech. She did not know Miss Eastwich as we others did; did not know how her persistent silence had built a wall round her—a wall that no one dared to break down with the commonplaces of talk, or the littlenesses of mere human relationship. Miss Eastwich's silence had taught us to treat her as a machine; and as other than a machine we never dreamed of treating her.

But the youngest of us had seen Miss Eastwich for the first time that day. She was young, crude, ill-balanced, subject to blind, calf-like impulses. She was also the heiress of a rich tallow-chandler, but that has nothing to do with this part of the story. She jumped up from the hearth-rug, her unsuitably rich silk lace trimmed dressing gown falling back from her thin collarbones, and ran to the door and put an arm round Miss Eastwich's prim, lisse-encircled neck. I gasped. I should as soon have dared to embrace Cleopatra's Needle. 'Come in,' said the youngest of us - 'come in and get warm. There's lots of cocoa left.' She drew Miss Eastwich in and shut the door.

The vivid light of pleasure in the housekeeper's pale eyes went through my heart like a knife. It would have been so easy to put an arm round her neck, if one had only thought she wanted an arm there. But it was not I who had thought that—and indeed, my arm might not have brought the light evoked by the thin arm of the youngest of us.

'Now,' the youngest went on eagerly, 'you shall have the very biggest, nicest chair, and the cocoa pot's here on the hob as hot as hot—and we've all been telling ghost stories, only we don't believe in them a bit and when you get warm you ought to tell one too.'

Miss Eastwich—that model of decorum and decently done duties—tell a ghost story!

'You're sure I'm not in your way,' Miss Eastwich said, stretching her hands to the blaze. I wondered whether housekeepers have fires in their rooms even at Christmas time. 'Not a bit'—I said it, and I hope I said it as warmly as I felt it. 'I—Miss Eastwich—I'd have asked you to come in other times—only I didn't think you'd care for girls' chatter.'

The third girl, who was really of no account, and that's why I have not said anything about her before, poured cocoa for our guest. I put my fleecy Madeira shawl round her shoulders. I could not think of anything else to do for her, and I found myself wishing desperately to do something.

The smiles she gave us were quite pretty. People can smile prettily at forty or fifty, or even later, though girls don't realise this. It occurred to me, and this was another knife-thrust, that I had never seen Miss Eastwich smile—a real smile, before. The pale smiles of dutiful acquiescence were not of the same blood as this dimpling, happy, transfiguring look.

'This is very pleasant,' she said, and it seemed to me that I had never before heard her real voice. It did not please me to think that at the cost of cocoa, a fire, and my arm round her neck, I might have heard this new voice any time these six years.

'We've been telling ghost stories,' I said. 'The worst of it is, we don't believe in ghosts. No one knows has ever seen one.'

'It's always what somebody told somebody, who told somebody you know,' said the youngest of us, 'and you can't believe that, can you?'

'What the soldier said, is not evidence,' said Miss Eastwich. Will it be believed that the little Dickens quotation pierced one more keenly than the new smile or the new voice?

'And all the ghost stories are so beautifully rounded off—a murder committed on the spot—or a hidden treasure, or a warning...I think that makes them harder to believe. The most horrid ghost story I ever heard was one that was quite silly.'

'Tell it.'

'I can't—there's nothing to tell. Miss Eastwich ought to tell one.'

'Oh do,' said the youngest of us, and her salt cellars loomed dark, as she stretched her neck eagerly and laid an entreating arm on our guest's knee.

'The only thing that I ever knew of was—was hearsay,' she said slowly, 'till just the end.'

I knew she would tell her story, and I knew she had never before told it, and I knew she was only telling it now because she was proud, and this seemed the only way to pay for the fire and the cocoa, and the laying of that arm round her neck.

'Don't tell it,' I said suddenly. 'I know you'd rather not.'

'I daresay it would bore you,' she said meekly, and the youngest of us, who after all, did not understand everything, glared resentfully at me.

'We should just love it,' she said. 'Do tell us. I'm certain anything you think ghostly would be quite too beautifully horrid for anything.'

Miss Eastwich finished her cocoa and reached up to set the cup on the mantelpiece.

'I can't do any harm,' she said half to herself, 'they don't believe in ghosts, and it wasn't exactly a ghost either. And they're all over twenty—they're not babies.'

There was a breathing time of hush and expectancy. The fire crackled and the gas suddenly flared higher because the billiard lights had been put out. We heard the steps and voices of the men going along the corridors.

'It is really hardly worth telling,' Miss Eastwich said doubtfully, shading her faded face from the fire with her thin hand.

We all said 'Go on—oh, go on—do!'

'Well,' she said, 'twenty years ago—and more than that—I had two friends, and I loved them more than anything in the world. And they married each other—' She paused, and I knew just in what way she had loved each of them. The youngest of us said—'How awfully nice for you. Do go on.'

She patted the youngest's shoulder, and I was glad that I had understood, and that the youngest of all hadn't. She went on.

'Well, after they were married, I did not see much of them for a year or two; and then he wrote and asked me to come and stay, because his wife was ill, and I should cheer her up, and cheer him up as well; for it was a gloomy house, and he himself was growing gloomy too.'

I knew, as she spoke, that she had every line of that letter by heart. 'Well, I went. The address was in Lee, near London; in those days there were streets and streets of new villa-houses growing up round old brick mansions standing in their own grounds, with red walls round, you know, and a sort of flavour of coaching days, and post chaises, and Blackheath highwaymen about them. He had said the house was gloomy, and it was called 'The Firs', and I imagined my cab going through a dark, winding shrubbery, and drawing up in front of one of these sedate, old, square houses. Instead, we drew up in front of a large, smart villa, with iron railings, gay encaustic tiles leading from the iron gate to the stained-glass-panelled door, and for shrubbery only a few stunted cypresses and aucubas in the tiny front garden. But inside it was all warm and welcoming. He met me at the door.'

She was gazing into the fire, and I knew she had forgotten us. But the youngest girl of all still thought it was to us she was telling her story.

'He met me at the door,' she said again, 'and thanked me for coming, and asked me to forgive the past.'

'What past?' said that high priestess of the *inàpropos,* the youngest of all.

'Oh—I suppose he meant because they hadn't invited me before, or something,' said Miss Eastwich worriedly, 'but it's a very dull story, I find, after all, and—'

'Do go on,' I said—then I kicked the youngest of us, and got up to rearrange Miss Eastwich's shawl, and said in blatant dumb show, over the shawled shoulder 'Shut up, you little idiot—'

After another silence, the housekeeper's new voice went on.

'They were very glad to see me, and I was very glad to be there. You girls, now, have such troops of friends, but these two were all I had—all I had ever had. Mabel wasn't exactly ill, only weak and excitable. I thought he seemed more ill than she did. She went to bed early and before she went, she asked me to keep him company through his last pipe, so we went into the dining room and sat in the two armchairs on each side of the fireplace. They were covered with green leather I remember. There were bronze groups of horses and a black marble clock on the mantelpiece—all wedding presents. He poured out some whisky for himself, but he hardly touched it. He sat looking into the fire. At last I said: 'What's wrong? Mabel looks as well as you could expect.'

'He said, 'Yes—but I don't know from one day to another that she won't begin to notice something wrong. That's why I wanted you to come. You were always so sensible and strong-minded, and Mabel's like a little bird on a flower.'

'I said yes, of course, and waited for him to go on. I hought he must be in debt, or in trouble of some sort. So I just waited. Presently he said:

'Margaret, this is a very peculiar house'—he always called me Margaret. You see we'd been such old friends. I told him I thought the house was very pretty, and fresh, and homelike—only a little too new—but that fault would mend with time. He said:

'It *is* new: that's just it. We're the first people who've ever lived in it. If it were an old house, Margaret, I should think it was haunted.'

'I asked if he had seen anything. 'No,' he said 'not yet.'

'Heard then?' said I.

'No—not heard either,' he said, 'but there's a sort of feeling: I can't describe it—I've seen nothing and I've heard nothing, but I've been so near to seeing and hearing, just near, that's all. And something follows me about—only when I turn round, there's never anything, only my shadow. And I always feel that I *shall* see the thing next minute—but I never do—not quite—it's always just not visible.'

'I thought he'd been working rather hard—and tried to cheer him up by making light of all this. It was just nerves, I said. Then he said he had thought I could help him, and did I think anyone he had wronged could have laid a curse on him, and did I believe in curses. I said I didn't—and the only person anyone could have said he had wronged forgave him freely, I knew, if there was anything to forgive. So I told him this too.'

It was I, not the youngest of us, who knew the name of that person, wronged and forgiving. 'So then I said he ought to take Mabel away from the house and have a complete change. But he said no; Mabel had got everything in order, and he could never manage to get her away just now without explaining everything—'and, above all,' he said, 'she mustn't guess there's anything wrong. I daresay I shan't feel quite such a lunatic now you're here.'

'So we said goodnight.'

'Is that all the story!' said the third girl, striving to convey that even as it stood it was a good story.

'That's only the beginning,' said Miss Eastwich. 'Whenever I was alone with him he used to tell me the same thing over and over again, and at first when I began to notice things, I tried to think that it was his talk that had upset my nerves. The odd thing was that it wasn't only at night—but in broad daylight—and particularly on the stairs and passages. On the staircase the feeling used to be so awful that I have had to bite my lips till they bled to keep myself from running upstairs at full speed. Only I knew if I did I should go mad at the top. There was always something behind me—exactly as he had said—something that one could just not see. And a sound that one could just not hear. There was a long corridor at the top of the house. I have sometimes almost seen something—you know how one sees things without looking—but if I turned round, it seemed as if the thing drooped and melted into my shadow. There was a little window at the end of the corridor.

'Downstairs there was another corridor, something like it, with a cupboard at one end and the kitchen at the other. One night I went down into the kitchen to heat some milk for Mabel. The servants had gone to bed. As I stood by the fire, waiting for the milk to boil, I glanced through the open door and along the passage. I never could keep my eyes on what I was doing in that house. The cupboard door was partly open; they used to keep empty boxes and things in it. And, as I looked, I knew that now it was not going to be 'almost' any more.

Yet I said, 'Mabel?' not because I thought it could be Mabel who was crouching down there, half in and half out of the cupboard. The thing was grey at first, and then it was black, and when I whispered, 'Mabel,' it seemed to sink down till it lay like a pool of ink on the floor, and then its edges drew in, and it seemed to flow, like ink when you tilt up the paper you have spilt it on; and it flowed into the cupboard till it was all gathered into the shadow there. I saw it go quite plainly. The gas was full on in the kitchen. I screamed aloud, but even then, I'm thankful to say, I had enough sense to upset the boiling milk, so that when he came downstairs three steps at a time, I had the excuse for my scream of a scalded hand. The explanation satisfied Mabel, but next night he said:

' 'Why didn't you tell me? It was that cupboard. All the horror of the house comes out of that. Tell me—have you seen anything yet? Or is it only the nearly seeing and nearly hearing still?'

'I said, 'You must tell me first what you've seen. He told me, and his eyes wandered, as he spoke, to the shadows by the curtains, and I turned up all three gas lights, and lit the candles on the mantelpiece. Then we looked at each other and said we were both mad, and thanked God that Mabel at least was sane. For what he had seen was what I had seen.

'After that I hated to be alone with a shadow, because at any moment I might see something that would crouch, and sink, and lie like a black pool, and then slowly draw itself into the shadow that was nearest. Often that shadow was my own. The thing came first at night, but afterwards there was no hour safe from it. I saw it at dawn and at noon, in the firelight, and always it crouched and sank, and was a pool that flowed into some shadow and became part of it.

And always I saw it with a straining of the eyes—a pricking and aching. It seemed as though I could only just see it, as if my sight, to see it, had to be strained to the uttermost. And still the sound was in the house—the sound that I could just not hear. At last, one morning early, I did hear it. It was close behind me, and it was only a sigh. It was worse than the thing that crept into the shadows.

'I don't know how I bore it. I couldn't have borne it, if I hadn't been so fond of them both. But I knew in my heart that, if he had no one to whom he could speak openly, he would go mad, or tell Mabel. His was not a very strong character; very sweet, and kind, and gentle, but not strong.

He was always easily led. So I stayed on and bore up, and we were very cheerful, and made little jokes, and tried to be amusing when Mabel was with us. But when we were alone, we did not try to be amusing. And sometimes a day or two would go by without our seeing or hearing anything, and we should perhaps have fancied that we had fancied what we had seen and heard—only there was always the feeling of there being something about the house, that one could just not hear and not see. Sometimes we used to try not to talk about it, but generally we talked of nothing else at all.

And the weeks went by, and Mabel's baby was born. The nurse and the doctor said that both mother and child were doing well. He and I sat late in the dining-room that night. We had neither of us seen or heard anything for three days; our anxiety about Mabel was lessened. We talked of the future—it seemed then so much brighter than the past. We arranged that, the moment she was fit to be moved, he should take her away to the sea, and I should superintend the moving of their furniture into the new house he had already chosen. He was gayer than I had seen him since his marriage—almost like his old self. When I said goodnight to him, he said a lot of things about my having been a comfort to them both. I hadn't done anything much, of course, but still I am glad he said them.

'Then I went upstairs, almost for the first time without that feeling of something following me. I listened at Mabel's door. Everything was quiet. I went on towards my own room, and in an instant I felt that there *was* something behind me. I turned. It was crouching there; it sank, and the black fluidness of it seemed to be sucked under the door of Mabel's room.

I went back. I opened the door a listening inch. All was still. And then I heard a sigh close behind me. I opened the door and went in. The nurse and the baby were asleep. Mabel was asleep too—she looked so pretty —like a tired child—the baby was cuddled up into one of her arms with its tiny head against her side. I prayed then that Mabel might never know the terrors that he and I had known. That those little ears might never hear any but pretty sounds, those clear eyes never see any but pretty sights. I did not dare to pray for a long time after that. Because my prayer was answered. She never saw, never heard anything more in this world. And now I could do nothing more for him or for her.

'When they had put her in her coffin, I lighted wax candles round her, and laid the horrible white flowers that people will send near her, and then I saw he had followed me. I took his hand to lead him away. 'At the door we both turned. It seemed to us that we heard a sign. He would have sprung to her side, in I don't know what mad, glad hope. But at that instant we both saw it. Between us and the coffin, first grey, then black, it crouched an instant, then sank and liquefied—and was gathered together and drawn till it ran into the nearest shadow. And the nearest shadow was the shadow of Mabel's coffin. I left the next day. His mother came. She had never liked me.'

Miss Eastwich paused. I think she had quite forgotten us.

'Didn't you see him again?' asked the youngest of us all.

'Only once,' Miss Eastwich answered, 'and something black crouched then between him and me. But it was only his second wife, crying beside the coffin. It's not a cheerful story is it? And it doesn't lead anywhere. I've never told anyone else. I think it was seeing his daughter that brought it all back.'

She looked towards the dressing room door.

'Mabel's baby?'

'Yes—and exactly like Mabel, only with his eyes.'

The youngest of all had Miss Eastwich's hands, and was petting them.

Suddenly the woman wrenched her hands away, and stood at her gaunt height, her hands clenched, eyes straining. She was looking at something that we could not see, and I know what the man in the Bible meant when he said: 'The hair of my flesh stood up.'

What she saw seemed not quite to reach the height of the dressing room door handle. Her eyes followed it down, down—widening and widening. Mine followed them—all the nerves of them seemed strained to the uttermost—and I almost saw—or did I quite see? I can't be certain. But we all heard the long drawn, quivering sigh. And to each of us it seemed to be breathed just behind us.

It was I who caught up the candle—it dripped all over my trembling hand—and was dragged by Miss Eastwich to the girl who had fainted during the second extra. But it was the youngest of all whose lean arms were round the housekeeper when we turned away, and that have been round her many a time since, in the new home where she keeps house for the youngest of us.

The doctor who came in the morning said that Mabel's daughter had died of heart disease— which she had inherited from her mother. It was that that had made her faint during the second extra. But I have sometimes wondered whether she may not have inherited something from her father. I have never been able to forget the look on her dead face.